DATE DUE

25|4|D			

Estelle

Annabelle Starr

EGMONT

Special thanks to:

Rachel Rimmer, St John's Walworth Church of England
School and Belmont Primary School

EGMONT
We bring stories to life

Published in Great Britain 2007
by Egmont UK Limited
239 Kensington High Street, London W8 6SA

Text & illustrations © 2007 Egmont UK Ltd
Text by Rachel Rimmer
Illustrations by Helen Turner

ISBN 978 1 4052 3248 7

1 3 5 7 9 10 8 6 4 2

A CIP catalogue record for this title is available
from the British Library

Typeset by Avon DataSet Ltd, Bidford on Avon, Warwickshire
Printed and bound in Great Britain by the CPI Group

'These books are brilliant! I'm definitely going to tell my friends about them cos they'll love them too'
Ellie, age 11

'I love the girl-speak, the mobile-phone chats and the fact files'
Nina, age 10

'I loved the pages at the beginning of the books – they really helped me to get into the characters'
Rebecca, age 9

'Exciting and quite unpredictable. I like that the girls do the detective work'
Lauren, age 10

'They make you want to read on, and the stories are very descriptive'
Krystyna, age 9

We want to know what *you* think about *Megastar Mysteries*! Visit:

www.mega-star.co.uk

for loads of coolissimo megastar stuff to do!

Meet the
Megastar Mysteries Team!

Hi, this is me, **Rosie Parker** (otherwise known as Nosy Parker), and these are my best mates . . .

. . . **Soph** (Sophie) **McCoy** – she's a real fashionista sista – and . . .

. . . **Abs** (Abigail) **Flynn**, who's officially une grande genius.

Here's my mum, **Liz Parker**. Much to my embarrassment, her fashion and music taste is well and truly stuck in the 1980s (but despite all that I still love her dearly) . . .

. . . and my nan, **Pam Parker**, the murder-mystery freak I mentioned on the cover. Sometimes, just sometimes, her crackpot ideas do come in handy.

Consider yourself introduced!

Rosie's Mini Megastar Phrasebook

Want to speak our lingo, but don't know your soeurs from your signorinas? No problemo! Just use my comprehensive guide . . .

-a-rama	add this ending to a word to indicate a large quantity: e.g. 'The after-show party was celeb-a-rama'
amigo	Spanish for 'friend'
au contraire, mon frère	French for 'on the contrary, my brother'
au revoir	French for 'goodbye'
barf/barfy/barfissimo	sick/sick-making/very sick-making indeed
bien sûr, ma soeur	French for 'of course, my sister'
bon	French for 'good'
bonjour	French for 'hello'
celeb	short for 'celebrity'
convo	short for 'conversation'
cringe-fest	a highly embarrassing situation
Cringeville	a place we all visit from time to time when something truly embarrassing happens to us
cringeworthy	an embarrassing person, place or thing might be described as this
daggy	Australian for 'unfashionable' or unstylish'
doco	short for 'documentary'
exactamundo	not a real foreign word, but a great way to express your agreement with someone
exactement	French for 'exactly'

excusez moi	French for 'excuse me'
fashionista	'a keen follower of fashion' – can be teamed with 'sista' for added rhyming fun
glam	short for 'glamorous'
gorge/gorgey	short for 'gorgeous': e.g. 'the lead singer of that band is gorge/gorgey'
hilarioso	not a foreign word at all, just a great way to liven up 'hilarious'
hola, señora	Spanish for 'hello, missus'
hottie	no, this is *not* short for hot water bottle – it's how you might describe an attractive-looking boy to your friends
-issimo	try adding this ending to English adjectives for extra emphasis: e.g. coolissimo, crazissimo – très funissimo, non?
je ne sais pas	French for 'I don't know'
je voudrais un beau garçon, s'il vous plaît	French for 'I would like an attractive boy, please'
journos	short for 'journalists'
les Français	French for, erm, 'the French'
Loserville	this is where losers live, particularly evil school bully Amanda Hawkins
mais	French for 'but'
marvelloso	not technically a foreign word, just a more exotic version of 'marvellous'
massivo	Italian for 'massive'
mon amie/mes amis	French for 'my friend'/'my friends'
muchos	Spanish for 'many'

non	French for 'no'
nous avons deux garçons ici	French for 'we have two boys here'
no way, José!	'that's never going to happen!'
oui	French for 'yes'
quelle horreur!	French for 'what horror!'
quelle surprise!	French for 'what a surprise!'
sacré bleu	French for 'gosh' or even 'blimey'
stupido	this is the Italian for 'stupid' – stupid!
-tastic	add this ending to any word to indicate a lot of something: e.g. 'Abs is braintastic'
très	French for 'very'
swoonsome	decidedly attractive
si, si, signor/signorina	Italian for 'yes, yes, mister/miss'
terriblement	French for 'terribly'
une grande	French for 'a big' – add the word 'genius' and you have the perfect description of Abs
Vogue	it's only the world's most influential fashion magazine, darling!
voilà	French for 'there it is'
what's the story, Rory?	'what's going on?'
what's the plan, Stan?	'which course of action do you think we should take?'
what the crusty old grandads?	'what on earth?'
zut alors!	French for 'darn it!'

Hi Megastar reader!

My name's Annabelle Starr*. I'm a fashion stylist – just like Soph's Aunt Penny – which means it's my job to help celebrities look their best at all times.

Over the years, I've worked with all sorts of big names, some of whom also have seriously big egos! Take the time I flew all the way to Japan to style a shoot for a girl band. One of the members refused to wear the designer number I'd picked out for her and insisted on sporting a dress her mum had run up from some revolting old curtains instead. The only way I could get her to take it off was to persuade her it didn't match her pet Pekinese's outfit!

Anyway, when I first started out, I never dreamt I'd write a series of books based around my crazy celebrity experiences, but that's just what I've done with Megastar Mysteries. Rosie, Soph and Abs have just the sort of adventures I wish my friends and I could have got up to when we were teenagers!

I really hope you enjoy reading the books as much as I enjoyed writing them!

Love **Annabelle**

* I'll let you in to a little secret: this isn't my real name, but in this business you can never be too careful!

Chapter One

'Mmm, pizza is yumissimo,' I said, grabbing my fourth slice from the mound of food that completely covered the kitchen table.

'If you want any garlic bread, you'd better be quick,' Abs warned, as she piled some on to her plate.

'Oi! Leave me some, Abs!' said Soph. 'Got a vampire on your case or something?'

We were at Soph's house, it was Saturday night, and we were doing what we do best – watching a reality-TV show and commenting on all the contestants. Soph's parents were out at a party, so she'd invited us round. Normally, we took turns going to each other's houses at the weekend.

I mean, we couldn't always be at my house, that was for sure. We'd all be driven slowly mad. Not only would my nan not let us watch what we wanted to (unless it happened to be a murder-mystery programme), but Mum would probably insist on inflicting her terrible taste in music on us. Seriously, the last time Abs and Soph set foot in the Parker household, they were scarred for life. Mum came into the room wearing disgustissimo leggings that caused Soph to have a serious fashion spasm, and Nan chuntered on and on about how great *Inspector Morse* is for so long that Abs nearly died of boredom. Sooo embarrassing!

Anyway, Soph's house is coolissimo to say the least. Her parents are pretty loaded, so they've got lots of très nice stuff. There's an amazing L-shaped leather sofa that's the size of a small island, and a seriously slick plasma TV. Soph's bedroom is way bigger than my lounge at home. Funny thing is though, Soph doesn't really notice stuff like that. She's definitely not snobby about it (unlike some people at school – like my arch enemy Amanda Hawkins), but what Soph *will* notice is what you're wearing. Example:

Soph: *Rosie, you've had that T-shirt for three years!*
Me: *So?*
Soph: *I can't believe you haven't done something with it. You know, like, customised it or something.*
Me: *Last time I tried that I ended up with an outfit that Mum loved – it was sooo not a good look.*
Abs: *Why don't you do something creative to it, Soph?*
Me: *Oh, no. No way, José. I am perfectly happy with it as it is. It's green, it has the words 'Rock Chick' on it – that's cool, isn't it?*
Soph: *Au contraire, mon frère. First, you are sooo NOT a rock chick. Second, it looks worn-*

in now, so you should fray up the edges to make it look a bit cooler. Third, you could maybe wear it with a skirt. Something other than jeans, anyway.

You see? Soph thinks she knows everything about clothes. And everything about the person who wears them. Well, OK, she does know a lot about me. We've been mates, like, forever. But you'd think by now she'd have got that even though I like clothes, I just don't care about fashion the way she does.

'Quick! *Stage-Struck*'s starting!' yelled Abs, who'd wandered back into the lounge during this thrilling discussion between me and Soph (she's only heard it about a million times before).

Me and Soph grabbed the last bits of garlic bread and raced into the lounge to take up our positions, me on the left, nearest the door. Dunno why, but I always have to be near the door. Maybe it's some kind of survival instinct I've got from living with my family – I often have to escape up to my room to keep my sanity. Like the time Mum and Nan got into this argument about who was more attractive – George Michael in his Wham! days or Detective Inspector Frost. They are totally nuts. Obviously the answer was neither. I started to worry that the inability to spot hotness was genetic, so I had to go upstairs and gaze at my Fusion posters to check that, yes, Maff, the lead singer, was still absolutely gorge.

Anyway, Abs always sits in the middle, near the remote controls. She likes to be the one to use them, even if it's not her house. And Soph always sits in the corner of the 'L' bit of the sofa. I mean, it's not exactly comfy on the bum, but she likes being different. Still, we can all see the telly from our positions, so it works for us. This was the first episode of a show searching for the star for a new musical called *High Kickin'* premiering in London's West End later in the year, so it was important that we saw every detail. There were two big parts up for grabs – one male and one female – but there could only be one winner, so whichever part was left over would go to a professional.

'And now, let's meet the judges on our panel,' the totally glitzed-up TV presenter, Daisy Finnegan, said. 'Anna Potter, the choreographer!'

'She's très strict,' Abs said.

'Yeah, but fair,' I pointed out.

'Next, we have the actor and singer, Michael Donovan!'

'I'm loving his shirt/tie combo,' Soph said.

'What, yellow and purple?' I asked. *Gross.*

'Yeah, it's bold, it's bright –'

'It's barfissimo,' Abs finished.

'And, finally, we have the famous director of musicals, the man who will make this winner a star, Jeff Dalglish!' The presenter cooed at Jeff, who waved to the audience and the camera.

'Actually, he's not bad looking,' Soph said.

'Yeah,' I agreed. 'And he knows it.'

'And now let's see just how many people want to be a West End star!' the presenter cried. Then they cut to this film of people queuing up outside lots of different theatres and singing for the cameras. A doddery old man was doing a little tap dance routine and there was even one woman dressed as Mary Poppins. I mean, the lengths some people will go to just to get on telly!

'Hmmm. It's not going to be hard to whittle this lot down to only a few good 'uns,' I said.

'Oooh, harsh!' Abs said. 'Lucky you're not on the panel.'

'Au contraire, mon frère. I would be the voice of reason. I'd be no-nonsense, straight talking and full of kind advice. Like "Just stop singing already!"'

'Sssh. They're auditioning now,' Soph hissed, scanning the hopefuls' outfits. 'Seriously – have these people never heard of *Vogue*?'

For the next half hour we had a très fab time watching people embarrass themselves by attempting to sing, dance and – well, do *anything* in time to some music. Oh, the joys of reality TV! What the crusty old grandads did people watch before this?

'Tune in next week, when we'll have the first round of contestants singing live in the studio, and

you can vote for your favourite,' the presenter said.

'Unless it's fixed from the start,' said Abs-the-cynic. 'You can tell the people they followed in this episode are going to go far. Like Estelle.'

'Yeah, well, she *was* brilliant,' I said.

'And she's got a cool look going on,' said Soph. 'Maybe I should dye my hair raven black.'

'Yes,' I said. '*Or* you could make it like Jerome's – all long, lank and greasy.'

'Mmm, yes, such a good look,' Abs said. 'He was special.'

Soph shuddered. 'No way, José. Although he could sing quite well . . .'

'Yeah, so can Estelle. *And* she's written some songs of her own,' I pointed out.

'That's not always a good thing,' Abs said. 'Did you hear that Ivan bloke and his so-called "show tune"?'

An hour later, when Soph's parents came back after their party, we'd worked our way through everyone. Estelle was definitely our favourite.

'Hi, girls,' Soph's mum said, as she walked into

the lounge. We whipped our feet off her posh coffee table. Mrs McCoy can be scary sometimes, but she's really très nice. 'Have a good evening?'

'Yes, thanks, Mrs M,' I said. 'You?'

'Yes, it was lovely. And I met someone rather interesting, Soph.'

'Oh, yeah?' Soph rolled her eyes and smirked at me and Abs.

'Your mother spent a very long time talking to him,' called Soph's dad from the kitchen.

Soph's mum looked a bit flustered. 'Oh, Richard, we were just *chatting*. He moved to Borehurst last week so I was telling him some stuff about the area.'

Soph sighed. 'I thought you said *interesting*, Mum.'

'Wait till you hear who it was,' her mother said. 'Jeff Dalglish.'

'What?!' the three of us shrieked.

'The judge on *Stage-Struck*?' Abs said.

'Yup. And he needs a babysitter next weekend. So I volunteered you, Soph.'

Soph leapt up and hugged her mum, then shouted, 'I'm going to his house! I'm going to his house!'

She flung herself at me and Abs and we all jumped up and down in a circle. Imagine! Soph babysitting for someone famous! Someone who'd been in the celeb mags so many times, I felt I knew his lounge really well already! After all, I don't just *flick* through *Star Secrets* magazine every week, y'know. No, siree. I remember every detail of every celeb shoot and interview they do. I carry a lot of interesting information around in my head, actually. For example, I know Jeff's wife, Melissa, is an actress. She was in one of those cop shows recently. And before that, she was a model. They met on a shoot for a magazine interview with Jeff. He had to have lots of women draped over him for the picture and Melissa was one of them. Since then, they've shown off their children (two) and happy home (gorgeous!) in various mags. And now Soph would be able to give me a first-hand account of what their new place was like!

'See, I *do* meet interesting people sometimes,' Soph's mum said, smiling. 'When Jeff asked me if I knew anyone who could do it at such short notice, I thought of you, Soph, of course. He hasn't got time to interview candidates, and he needs someone who's trustworthy.'

'This is sooo cool!' Soph said.

'I wish we could come too,' I said, wistfully. 'I'd love to see his new house.'

'Can we?' Abs asked. 'Do you think he'd mind? Three of us would be more responsible than one, after all.' That's what I love about Abs. She always comes up with convincing reasons to do stuff.

'Good thinking, Batgirl! He doesn't have to pay us,' I said. Soph nudged me hard with her elbow. 'Well, he could pay *Soph*, of course . . .'

'Si, si, it would be so cool if you could come too,' Soph said. 'Imagine hanging out at the Dalglishs' house! Mum, d'you reckon he'd let us?'

'Well, I don't know. I can ask him, I suppose,' Mrs McCoy said slowly. 'I've got his number . . .'

'You've got his number?' I cried. 'Coolissimo!'

Soph's dad came into the lounge with two cups of coffee and shook his head at the sight of us all jumping up and down. 'I'd wait a bit before you call him,' he advised. 'The sound of all this shrieking won't encourage him to say yes.'

'No, call him now, Mum!' Soph said. 'While he's all pleased at having met such a nice person from Borehust. Go on, go on, go on.'

'Oh, all right then,' her mum said, going to the phone.

Me, Abs and Soph all grinned at each other and stood there, waiting to hear what he'd say.

I grabbed Abs's hand for luck.

'Hello, Jeff? Yes, it's Mary McCoy. We just met at the Walkers' party . . . Yes, that's right . . . No, she can still babysit. But we were wondering if her friends Abigail and Rosie could help her? . . . Yes, they're experienced babysitters, too . . . I've known them for years. Very nice girls . . . We thought three would be better than one . . . OK, great! We'll let you know. Thanks! . . . OK, here she is.' Soph's mum gestured for Soph to come to the phone. Putting her hand over it, she whispered, 'He said it's all right as long as your parents are happy about it.'

Yes!!! Abs and I high-fived and did a victory dance. We would definitely be able to convince our parents it was fine.

'Yes, sure,' Soph was saying. 'Thanks, Mr Dalglish . . . I can't wait to watch the show in your house! . . . Wow! Thanks! . . . Yes, see you next week.' She put the phone down and grinned at me and Abs. 'He says he'll see us next week at five and he'll get in loads of snacks for us!'

Wow! We were going to the house of a famous director and a model-turned-actress next week! Celeb heaven! And, if he gave us a bumper bag of sweets and treats, chocolate heaven too! What could be better?

Chapter Two

Monday mornings suck. I mean, who on earth invented them? Why ruin a perfectly good morning by forcing us to get out of bed and go to school? Not to mention having maths first thing. I think Abs is the sole person in the universe who actually *enjoys* Monday mornings, and that's only because she gets all the answers right and actually gets a kick out of working them out. Seriously. Sometimes I worry.

Anyway, this Monday morning was different. I was desperate to see Soph and Abs to talk about going to the Dalglishes' house and to tell them what I'd read about Jeff in last week's issue of *Star Secrets*. I'd remembered there'd been an article on him, so I'd delved into our recycling box, ferreting through old copies of *Unsolved Crimes* magazine and loads of empty jam jars, until I found it. Nan's got this thing about recycling now, and she's incorporated it into her cleaning routine. Anything that can be recycled gets chucked in the special bin – even if you haven't finished reading it yet. She's been known to wrest *Star Secrets* from my actual hands. Honestly, it's like living in a mad house sometimes. Recycling is great, don't get me wrong but, like I said to Nan, you're supposed to *finish* using something first and *then* pass it on. She just tutted at me as if I was personally responsible for global warming.

'So, what's the plan, Stan?' I asked Soph as soon as I got into our form room. I knew that she'd probably spent the whole of Sunday thinking about going to the Dalglishes' house too.

'Well, I thought we could arrive early, you

know, to prove we're très reliable, and also to get to talk to Jeff for as long as possible before he goes,' she said.

'Yeah, it's going to be a bit weird being in a celeb's house without the actual celeb being there,' I said.

'But that's the whole point – we're babysitting because they're not there,' Soph said, confused.

'I know, Soph, but I was just saying . . . oh, never mind.'

Luckily, Abs walked in at that moment. Sanity!

'Hi, girls,' she said. 'Cracked that algebra homework?'

Or maybe no sanity at all.

'Er, hello?' I said. 'Might I draw your attention to the very important event that is happening this Saturday? I have some inside goss for you about Jeff.'

'From *Star Secrets*?' said Abs, looking at the magazine I was now waving about. We don't call her clever for nothing.

'Yeah. Now listen –'

Just then, our gorgey form teacher, Mr Adams, walked in. 'Settle down, everyone,' he said. 'Time to take the register. Miss Flynn, shouldn't you be in your form room?'

'Yes sir, sorry, sir,' Abs said. 'Catch you at lunch,' she whispered as she left.

I nodded. They were going to love it!

* * *

That lunchtime, we grabbed some 'food', or what passes for it in our school canteen anyway, and huddled together on a table near the door. I pulled out *Star Secrets* again.

'Right. So, it turns out that Jeff had a sad and rocky childhood,' I said.

'Poor Jeff,' Soph said, biting into her sandwich.

'Yeah. His mother abandoned him and his sister when he was five, and then his dad died really soon after.'

'Oh, no!' Abs said.

I stabbed my finger at the spread with the interview on it. There was a picture of Jeff looking wistful (it made a change from him looking exasperated as yet another person proved they had no singing talent). I continued with the summary of the interview, 'So Jeff and his sister went into care, but became separated and he completely lost touch with her. He still doesn't know where she is or what happened to her.'

'How sad!' Soph and Abs said, leaning in towards me to hear the next bit.

'Well, that's it really. He thinks she might have gone to America with her adoptive family, but he doesn't know for sure.'

'So why was he telling *Star Secrets* all about it?' Abs asked. 'There've been loads of articles about him recently and none of them has mentioned it.'

'Well, apparently he's hoping some publicity about it might help him find her. He'd really like Oscar and Lily to meet their auntie. She was called Jane and she had an unusual birthmark on her forehead, near her hairline.' I jabbed my finger at my own head, to demonstrate.

'What kind of birthmark?' Soph asked, peering at my face in quite an unnerving way.

'A heart-shaped strawberry mark,' I read from the magazine.

'So poor Jeff Dalglish has lost his sister for, what? About thirty-five years, if he's forty now?' Abs said, putting those amazing maths skills to work.

'Yeah, pretty much. And his mother. He says he found it really hard to trust people after his troubled childhood – until he met Melissa,' I said.

'Aaaah!' the girls chorused.

'And now that he's got two children, he can't understand why a parent would abandon their child. Especially if that would mean them being separated, like him and Jane.'

'It's so sad,' Soph said.

'I bet loads of women come forward saying they're Jane,' said Abs-the-cynic. 'You know, now he's rich and famous.'

'Yeah, probably,' I said. 'That's a risk you run when you're a celebrity, I guess.'

Just then, Mr Lord appeared behind Abs. 'Jeff Dalglish, you say?' he said. 'I remember him when I was working on *The Showman*, all those years ago. Back when he wasn't famous and he wasn't rich, and it was all about the beauty of the drama and the craft of acting . . .'

Soph, Abs and I rolled our eyes at each other. Way to interrupt a conversation, Mr Lord. Oh yeah, and a *private* conversation at that. His voice was so loud, other people were turning round too.

'Were you in *The Snowman* – was that you singing, sir?' my arch-enemy Amanda Hawkins asked Mr Lord. The suck-up. She and her equally evil buddies, Lara and Keira, were now sitting on a table right behind us. Sacré bleu, did *everyone* have to listen to what we were saying?

Mr Lord looked a bit embarrassed. '*The Showman*, not *The Snowman* and er, no, I was working for the theatre. As an usher.' He coughed. 'But I was always talking to the actors, and they would always pass on tips to me. Tips that made my experience on *Doctor Who* such a fruitful one.

Tips about how to really *feel* a part, how to *be* a Cyberman . . .'

He was off again.

'Anyway,' said Soph, 'I'm really excited about meeting Jeff. Wasn't it nice of him to promise to buy us snacks?'

'Yeah,' I said, loudly, noticing that Amanda and her cronies were listening. Ha! An excellent opportunity to make them jealous. 'I can't believe we get to see their house!'

'And meet their cute kids!' Abs bellowed.

'It's just so cool that we're babysitting for the Dalglishes this weekend,' I shouted.

'He was so nice when I spoke to him on the *phone*,' Soph shouted back.

'No need to shout, girls,' Mr Lord said, finally realising we weren't listening to him any more. 'Keep that projection for the stage, Rosie.'

'Yes, sir, sorry, sir. I'm just so excited that I'm going to meet Jeff Dalglish this weekend!' I cried.

Mr Lord shook his head and wandered off towards the other teachers. Amanda, Lara and

Keira were glaring at us. They'd obviously heard every word. They were sitting right behind Soph, so unless they had totally disengaged their brains – which I wouldn't put past them – they couldn't have failed to work out what we were up to that weekend.

They got up and flounced off after Mr Lord in a flouncy way. Well, as flouncy as people who look as sour as if they've just eaten a basket of lemons *can* look.

Me, Soph and Abs cracked up. Only 12.30 and we'd already made Amanda Hawkins jealous. Turned out Mondays could be good after all.

Chapter Three

It was one of those loooong weeks. You know, when you're really looking forward to something and immediately time slows down and every single lesson feels like forever, and every evening stretches out for eternity and you feel you will NEVER get to the magic day. Well, this was one of those weeks.

However, *finally*, Saturday arrived. Soph was working in Dream Beauty, the salon where she has a weekend job, so it was only me and Abs texting each other all day:

Me: Can't believe it's Saturday!

Abs: I know!

Me: So are you going glam or casual?

Abs: Casual glam, I thought.

Me: Yeah, me too.

But what did that mean? Where was Soph when I needed her? Of course, we'd been discussing our wardrobes all week. She'd suggested a few options, and even lent me some stuff, but now I had only three hours before I was going to meet a celeb, I froze.

Me: T-shirt and skirt OK?

Abs: Si, si. Megan says you should wear pink.

Megan is Abs's five-year-old sister and she's going through a pink phase that seems to have lasted her whole life. She likes to tell us what to do when we go to Abs's house and wearing pink is usually her number-one command. Soph loves turning up in wacky colour combinations just to see Megan's face. She gets very strict about things like that. (Megan, that is, not Soph. Soph will wear any colour combo and make it work somehow. I don't know how she does it.)

Anyway, about a million years later, I was finally ready. Mum was going to take us all there, on her way to an eighties tribute-band show (which she insists on calling a gig). As per usual, she was wearing her revoltissimo dungarees (apparently they were fashionable in the eighties, but not even Soph – fashion queen supreme – can believe it), so I made Mum promise not to get out of the car at the Dalglishes' house.

'Well, maybe I should say hello. Mary said he was charming,' she said.

'Mum. Seriously. Just stay in the car. You'll be late for your "gig" otherwise. You don't have time to chat! Please?' I pleaded.

'Oh, OK. I'll have to meet him another time,' she said, putting some lipstick on anyway. 'Right, off we go. Abs first, is it?'

We got to the Dalglishes' house at five o'clock on the dot. Luckily we'd picked Soph up last – she was so nervous she was jiggling her legs about in the back seat, which drove me and Abs crazy. I suppose she was the main babysitter, so it was her reputation at stake. Not that she had anything to worry about. I mean, me and Abs are totally reliable. And we're totally cool about meeting celebs. Especially ones that are all over the papers, and present the biggest show on the telly at the moment.

It was a TRÈS nice house. They had a large gravel drive and trees in the front garden and there were two cars outside. Although Soph's house is nice, this knocked its socks off. If only I was doing an at-home exclusive for *Star Secrets* – I'd get to nose about in every room and talk to Melissa and Jeff about their happy life and gorgeous children, and I'd say something so witty and clever, they'd instantly warm to me and they'd insist I was in the photos too – their new best friend, in the magazine for all to see – and they'd invite me round the whole time . . .

'Hello, hello, welcome!' Jeff Dalglish called from his front door as we got out of the car.

'He's very nice looking! He reminds me of a young Simon Le Bon,' Mum whispered to me as I shut the car door. I frowned at her and then said loudly, 'Thanks, Mum. Bye!'

Jeff was standing in the hallway holding the door open, and a very small, dark-haired boy was peering round his leg. 'Come in!' Jeff said. 'You must be Sophie, right?' He stuck his hand out to Soph.

She shook it. 'Hello, yes, erm, hi. I'm Sophie, yes,' she said, a bit flustered.

'Hello, Mr Dalglish, I'm Abigail,' said Abs. I love Abs. She's so great with parents and teachers and people like that. Although she does make us look bad. She shook his hand and went into the hall.

I shot forward with my arm outstretched. 'Hi, Rosie. Um, I mean, I'm Rosie,' I gabbled, shaking his hand very fast. Great. *Well done, Rosie. How to look like an idiot in one easy step.*

The little boy giggled. 'Ringa ringa Rosie!' he said.

I crouched down. 'Hello there,' I said. 'And who are you?'

'Oscar. I'm free,' the boy replied.

'This is Oscar,' Jeff said. 'He's three.'

'Free and a *half*,' Oscar said, just remembering.

'Sorry, three and a *half*,' Jeff said, winking at us all. 'Right, come through and I'll show you where everything is. Including my daughter. Lily! Come and say hello to the babysitters!' he shouted.

Jeff led us into this humongous lounge with a huge plasma telly and massive sofas. 'I'm guessing this is where you'll spend most of your time,' he said, grinning.

'Oh, yeah, we're so excited about the next episode of *Stage-Struck*!' Soph said.

'Great! It should be interesting, I think,' Jeff said. 'We've got some good singers lined up!'

'And it's really live?' Abs asked.

'Yup,' he said, looking at his watch. 'In fact, I should go in five minutes. I can't be late! Right, let me give you a quick tour.'

Jeff took us into the large, sparkling kitchen.

It was so tidy and spotless I knew they never actually went in there normally – I mean, you walk into our kitchen and you can't move for piles of post, baskets of washing, plastic bags . . . Nan does her best – 'I'll just have a quick flick with the duster,' she says, practically every day – but she's up against Mum's belief that nothing is more important than practising her Bananarama songs and accompanying routines. Believe me, I've tried to fight that too, and it's a losing battle.

'Those are for you.' Jeff pointed out the snacks he'd bought us. Oooh, yum!

'Thanks, Mr Dalglish!' Soph said.

'Call me Jeff,' he said. 'Right, let's find that Lily girl. Where could she be?'

'I know!' Oscar shouted, running up the stairs. 'In her bedroom!'

Lily was indeed in her bedroom. She was playing with a doll. Abs went straight over to her. 'My sister Megan has one of those,' she said. 'Shall we comb her hair?'

Lily nodded seriously and Abs sat down with her.

'Bedtime is seven o'clock for both of them,' Jeff said. 'They'll tell you which stories they want you to read. And the bathroom is in here for their bath.' He opened the door next to Lily's room and Soph and I peered in.

'And for brushing our toofs,' Oscar said.

'Yes, and for brushing your teeth. Good boy,' Jeff said. 'Right, I must go. Have fun, everyone and be good, Oscar. Lily, be a good girl! See you in the morning.' He kissed Oscar's head and ran to kiss Lily. Then he dashed downstairs. Two minutes later, we heard the front door slam.

'Daddy's gone to work,' Lily said.

'Yes, that's right. And your mummy's working too, isn't she?' I said. Jeff had told Soph's mum that Melissa was on a film shoot that week, in Ireland.

'Yes. She's going to be an old lady,' Lily said, knowingly. 'On a horse.'

'Oh, is she?' Abs said. 'Now, what shall we do with dolly's hair?'

* * *

Two hours later, Oscar and Lily were tucked up in bed, bathed, their 'toofs' brushed and stories read. Melissa had called to say goodnight to them, and they were both asleep. We'd collapsed on the sofa.

'Who knew that looking after two small children was so tiring?' moaned Soph.

'Oh, come on, they were sweet!' I said.

'Yeah, you're just tired cos you've been on your feet all day,' Abs pointed out. 'Anyway, it's time for the snacks!'

'Good thinking, Batgirl!' I said, leaping up and running to the kitchen. I returned with a jumbo tub of ice cream (three spoons), some popcorn and some cola. Perfectissimo!

Meanwhile, Soph had worked out how to use the plasma telly and she found the right channel. *Stage-Struck* was just starting!

It was the first live show so the cameras spent ages panning round the studio audience. Everyone was holding banners supporting their favourite singer. There were twenty contestants and they were going to be knocked out week by week till there was one remaining – the winner! Jeff was going to produce *High Kickin'*, so whoever won – male or female – they'd end up working with him.

'Look, it's Jeff!' Soph said, pointing at the telly just in case we hadn't spotted the enormous picture of him filling the screen.

'It's so weird, us sitting in his house while he's there,' I said.

'Yeah – he was only here a few hours ago,' Abs said. 'He's definitely the nicest one out of the judges, isn't he? I wouldn't like to be babysitting for Anna Potter.'

'No, siree!' I said. 'I bet *she* wouldn't provide snacks.'

'Speaking of which,' Abs said, 'you seem to have drunk most of the cola, Rosie. Give us a bit.'

'Sorry,' I said. 'Actually, I'm just going for a wee. It's gone right through me.' Nan was a terrible influence on me. I sounded just like her.

'Lovely,' Soph said, sarcastically. 'Now, sssh. The first contestant's starting!'

Oh, no! I was going to miss part of the show!

I raced up the stairs to the bathroom as quickly as poss, leaving the door open for a quick getaway. From the loo I could see into Jeff and Melissa's bedroom. Jeff had left the door open just a bit, and I could see some photo frames on a bedside table.

It was just too tempting.

After I'd finished, I snuck into their room and tiptoed over to the photos. Wow. There was one of Melissa – looking stunning, of course – and a very cute one of Oscar and Lily playing on a beach. It looked like a très nice holiday – on a kind of tropical island. The third photo was black and white and looked a bit faded. It was of a little boy and a baby girl. They looked very sweet too. I picked it up to have a closer look, and realised there was some dirt on it. I rubbed my finger over the baby's head, but it didn't come off. Duh! It must be on the photo. Hang on a sec! A mark on a forehead? Where had I read that before? Sacré bleu! It must be the birthmark Jeff mentioned in his interview. This was his lost baby sister! Wow!

I looked at it again, thinking how cute they both looked, and then suddenly remembered the show on downstairs.

Without stopping to admire the lovely bed-spread, I ran back down to the lounge, hurling myself into my seat just as the second contestant – Estelle, our favourite! – took a deep breath, ready to sing. Phew! I'd hardly missed anything!

Chapter Four

A few weeks later, the competition was really hotting up. They were down to twelve contestants. Estelle was still in it and me, Soph and Abs were desperate for her to win.

'She's just so genuine,' Abs said, flinging her schoolbag over her shoulder.

'Yeah, and she works really hard,' Soph said. 'Like me!'

'What the crusty old grandads are you talking about!' I said. 'I hardly think you swanning about in Dream Beauty and then getting paid to sit and watch telly while some children sleep upstairs really compares to Estelle's life of flipping burgers day in, day out!'

'Au contraire, mon frère,' Soph said, sniffily. 'Mrs Blessing is always getting me to sweep up hair and make cups of tea and do manicures. I don't just swan about, you know. I work my fingers to the bone!'

'And what have you got?' I said, grabbing her hand. 'Yup. Bony fingers! Great advert for a manicurist.'

Abs and I started giggling as we walked out of the school gates. After a bit, Soph joined in.

'But seriously,' I said. 'If Estelle won this, she wouldn't have to work in that très dodgy burger joint any longer. And she and her mum would get to move.'

'Yeah,' Abs said. 'It's really sweet, the way she talks about her mum the whole time, but not in a faking-it-for-the-cameras kind of way.'

'Si, si, you can totally tell she appreciates how difficult it was for her mum to bring her up by herself,' I agreed, pausing at my bus stop.

'Yeah, it must have been tough,' Soph said. 'It's exhausting enough just babysitting!'

Abs and I rolled our eyes.

'Although it was a bit odd the other day when Daisy asked her whether she had any more family she'd like to send a message to,' Abs said.

'Yeah, she looked really shifty, didn't she?' I replied, remembering how I'd thought it was a bit strange at the time.

'She wouldn't make eye contact with Daisy – a classic body language sign,' Soph said, nodding her head.

'Of what?' Abs asked.

'Of lying. Or being uncomfortable about something.'

'Right,' I said. 'Thanks for enlightening us, oh wise one.'

Soph opened her mouth to reply, but just then my bus arrived.

'See ya later, alligator,' I said as I got on. The others waved.

An hour later, while I was staring at my French homework, Soph instant-messaged us:

FashionPolice: Jeff wants us to babysit again!

NosyParker: No way, José!

FashionPolice: Si, si, signor. This Saturday. He rang my mum to ask.

CutiePie: I hope she said yes!

FashionPolice: Yup. And get this: he wants us to go to the show with him and look after the kids there!!!

NosyParker: You lie!

FashionPolice: Nope. Melissa's away working again so he needs us. And Oscar and Lily like us!

CutiePie: Coolissimo!!!

FashionPolice: Get your mums to call my mum to say it's OK to go to London with Jeff.

CutiePie: No problemo!
NosyParker: It HAS to be OK!!!

I raced downstairs to find Mum. She was in the kitchen, rifling through the cupboards.

'Oh, Rosie love, pass me that chopping board,' she said.

I handed it over. 'Mum, can I go to London and look after Lily and Oscar, please, while Jeff – you remember, their dad – is the judge on *Stage-Struck*, please? Please???'

'What?' Mum said. 'When?'

'This Saturday night. His wife's away again and he needs us to babysit, but in London.'

'This is the attractive one who looks like Simon le Bon, right?' Mum asked, beginning to chop an onion.

'Er, yes. You know, the celebrity judge!' I was dancing about in frustration at how slow she was being.

'Oh, yes. So you want to go with him to the show?'

I nodded my head furiously.

'Well, if Soph and Abs's mums say it's OK, it's OK with me,' she said. 'I guess you'll be safe with him. And it *is* your favourite show. I know you'd love to see it live!'

I hugged her tightly. 'Thanks, Mum! You're the best!'

'Am I?' she said. 'Well, how about helping me chop these onions then? I'm making onion soup.'

Oh, dear. Mum had decided to cook a 'proper meal'. I knew I should have stocked up on chocolate earlier.

* * *

The next day, Soph, Abs and I were très, très excited. It was Wednesday and in three days we'd be in London at the *Stage-Struck* studio!

'I hope we get to meet Estelle!' Abs said in the lunch queue.

'I am so going to talk to the person in charge of wardrobe,' Soph said. 'I mean, someone needs to stop putting poor Daisy Finnegan in those awful boots.' Daisy Finnegan, the presenter of *Stage-Struck*, had worn this pair of leather ankle boots twice now, and Soph was on a mission to stop her. 'Doesn't anyone notice they make her calves look enormous?' she kept wailing. 'Have these people never heard of *Vogue*?'

'I should think they have, and they're following its advice blindly,' Abs said.

'You sort them out, Soph!' I said encouragingly. 'We'll get Jeff to show us the person responsible.'

'If we're not too busy looking after Oscar and Lily,' Abs pointed out.

'Oh, they're so sweet, they won't mind,' Soph said airily.

'I can't believe we're going to babysit the Dalglishes' children again,' I said, grinning with glee. Not even the sight of limp, pale, overcooked broccoli on my plate could wipe the smile from my face.

Someone else could though. 'I can't believe you're going to babysit the Dalglishes' children either,' said a familiar voice behind me. 'Jeff and Melissa'd never let losers like you lot near their precious kids.'

I whirled round to see – surprise, surprise – Amanda Witchface Hawkins smiling at me in that très irritating and superior way of hers. I started to splutter, 'Shut up, Amanda, what do *you* know?'

'I know you live in a world of your own, Nosy Parker, and that sometimes you think your little celebrity fantasies are real.'

Abs pulled my arm. 'Ignore her,' she whispered. 'Let's sit down.'

I was still spluttering. 'What? What?' *Oh, good comeback, Rosie. Well done.*

'You're obviously inventing this whole babysitting thing. I mean, who would want *you* to look after their kids?!' Amanda and her cronies laughed. They were standing there cackling at me like, well, three witches. We should so do *Macbeth* next term. I'll have a word with Time Lord. He always gives Amanda the best parts anyway, so it'd be perfect.

'Oh, get over yourself, Amanda,' Abs said, grabbing me and leading me away.

'Get some help, Rosie! It's never too late!' Amanda shouted after me, laughing again.

'What is *with* her?' I asked as I sat down. Soph and Abs looked at me sympathetically.

'Let's not worry about Snore-kins Hawkins,' Soph said. 'She always talks rubbish – it's très dull.'

'That's a good name for her, actually,' I said, impressed. 'Nearly as good as Dork-Hawkins.' I'd taken to calling Amanda that – in my head – after Belle, the editor of *Star Secrets*, misheard me once.

Soph looked pleased. 'It's kind of a shame her name doesn't rhyme with "evil". If only her parents had called her "Weevil".'

'Evil Weevil Hawkins?' Abs said, giggling.

'Sounds good to me,' I muttered. 'Anyway, about Saturday. What's the story, Rory?' I asked, forgetting about Amanda and focusing on our celeb-tastic plans!

✳ ✳ ✳

That Saturday at five o'clock, we were at the Dalglishes' house again. Soph's mum dropped us off this time, hoping to say hi to Jeff, I think, but he didn't give her a chance. When he opened the door, he ushered us in really quickly, and then stuck his head outside to look around.

'My mum says hi,' Soph said, cautiously, in case he was wondering who the mad woman in the car was, waving at him furiously.

'What? Oh, er, right,' he said, closing the door and bolting it. We looked at each other, a bit startled.

'OK, the children are upstairs. If you could get them into their coats, we have to leave in five minutes,' Jeff said.

As we went upstairs, I looked round to see Jeff peering outside again through the hall window from behind the curtain. What *was* he looking for?

We found Oscar and Lily sitting on Lily's bed. Lily was combing Oscar's hair. He was sitting very still, with his eyes closed.

'We're in the hairdressers,' Lily said solemnly. 'I am the hairdresser.'

'I see,' Abs said. 'His hair looks very nice.'

Oscar opened his eyes and burst into a grin when he saw us. He wriggled off the bed and ran to hug our legs. 'Hello!' he said. 'You babysittin' nus 'gain?'

'Yes, we are!' I said, picking him up. 'But we're going in the car with Daddy first. So we have to put our coats on. Can you tell me where your coat lives?'

'My green one or my blue one or my red one?' Oscar asked. Good grief! How many coats did the child have? Oh, yes, he's the child of a model-turned-actress and a theatre producer. Of course he had billions of coats.

'Whichever one you want to wear,' Soph said. She's always pro freedom of expression when it comes to clothes.

'OK,' Oscar said happily.

Five minutes later, we were all in the hall, ready to go. Jeff was rushing round the house, double- and triple-checking that everything was locked and bolted and ready for the alarm.

'He seems très stressed,' I muttered to Abs.

'Well, the live shows *are* really stressful,' she said. 'And driving to London all the time can't help.'

'Plus his wife isn't around very much,' Soph whispered. 'Where is she this time anyway?'

'Dunno,' I said. 'Didn't your mum say?'

'Nope. Just that she was on another job.'

I was about to reply, when Jeff appeared again. 'Right, are we ready? Let's get in the car then. Come on! Come on!' he said.

We bundled the children and ourselves into Jeff's people-carrier. The kids had their own car seats – Lily even buckled herself in.

Jeff locked the house up and got into the driver's seat, next to Soph. 'We're late!' he said, annoyed. Me, Abs and Soph looked at each other nervously. Was he going to blame us? We'd arrived on time!

'Sorry?' Soph tried in a small voice.

'So-rry!' Oscar sang out.

Jeff reversed the car out of the drive. Then he

sighed. 'No, *I'm* sorry. There's no need for you lot to apologise.' He drove off, très fast. I clutched the armrest, glad I was buckled in. 'I've had a bit of a tough few weeks, to be honest,' he said.

'Is it cos of the show?' I asked, nervously.

'Well, that's quite tough, yes,' he said. 'It's a lot of time in London, which means I miss seeing these two.' He glanced at his kids in the rear-view mirror. 'But actually, it's because of that interview with *Star Secrets*.'

I gasped. Was he about to diss my favourite magazine?!

'Why? What's happened?' Abs asked, giving me a look meaning, 'Don't say anything!'

'Well, I don't know if you saw it, but I mentioned in that interview that I have a long-lost sister, Jane.'

We all nodded.

'Anyway, I now realise it was foolish to bring it up, because all I've had are nuisance calls from a woman who claims to be Jane. Literally dozens a day. Mostly to my office, but some to my mobile –

God knows how she got *that* number. It's driving me crazy.' He sighed again.

'That's awful,' Soph said.

'Yeah, it is,' Jeff replied. 'And she sounds absolutely loopy. I mean, seriously.' He glanced at Oscar and Lily again. 'I won't go into it now, but when I said I didn't believe her, she said . . . well, she said some dreadful things. Threats. I'm worried for these two.'

Abs and I looked at each other. How terrible!

'You really think she's crazy?' Abs asked.

'Yup,' Jeff said. 'And there's nothing the police can do. Apparently, she has to actually *do* something first before they can arrest her. It's ridiculous!' His voice cracked.

'Daddy?' Oscar said.

'Yes, darling?' Jeff struggled to sound normal.

'When's Mummy coming back?'

'Very soon,' Jeff said, soothingly. 'In three more sleeps.'

Oscar seemed satisfied with this, and put his thumb in his mouth.

'I know it's a bit mad to drive the children all the way to London and back,' Jeff said, 'but I need to know they're safe. Since Melissa's away, I can't leave them. That's why I need you three to look after them while I'm working. But if I know they're in the studio, I can set my mind at rest.'

'Do you think this woman knows your home address then?' Soph asked, a bit fearfully.

'No, not yet,' Jeff said. 'But I wouldn't put it past her. She keeps leaving messages that are horrible. I can avoid her calls but I can't help listening to the messages . . .'

I thought about it. If this woman was really Jane, why would she be so horrible to her long-lost brother? Why would she threaten his kids? Why would anyone do that unless they *were* truly unhinged. I shivered. This was definitely the dark side of being a celeb – weird people stalking you.

I suddenly remembered the photo I'd seen in Jeff and Melissa's bedroom. Surely there was one way to find out if she was telling the truth – check her birthmark.

'Jeff, I couldn't help noticing a photo in your house,' I began. 'A black-and-white one of a boy and a baby. Is it of you and Jane? Ow!' Abs had elbowed me in the ribs. She was giving me another one of her looks. I'm pretty sure this one said, 'Don't let him know you've been snooping round or he won't invite us back again!' After many years, I'm très good at interpreting Abs's expressions.

Luckily, Jeff laughed. 'I can tell nothing gets past you, Rosie!' he said.

'Rosie! Rosie!' Oscar sang. Lily burst into giggles.

'Um, yes, sorry,' I said. 'It caught my eye. It's a lovely photo.'

'It is, isn't it?' Jeff said, more serious now. 'Yes, it is me and Jane.'

'I saw the birthmark on her forehead – the one you mentioned in the interview,' I said.

'Yup. It's very distinctive,' Jeff said. 'In fact, one of my earliest memories is trying to scrub it off with a cloth and our dad telling me off.' His voice cracked again. I caught his eye in the rear-view mirror – he was welling up. He sniffed, then coughed. 'Right! Who wants to sing "The Wheels on the Bus"?!' he cried.

'Me!' shouted Lily.

'Me!' shouted Oscar.

'OK. Ready? One, two, three . . .'

As we all sang 'The Wheels on the Bus', me, Abs and Soph looked at each other. It was terrible to see Jeff Dalglish like this. He was normally so sure of himself, so relaxed. It was clear that this woman had really shaken him. And that he really wanted to find his sister. So far, it seemed like his search for her had brought him nothing but trouble. If only there was some way we could help him.

Chapter Five

When we got to the studio, Jeff was waved straight through the security barrier. We all had to sign in at reception. Lily and Oscar were really excited about their passes.

'That says "Lily" and that says "Oscar",' Lily explained, pointing to the stickers on their coats.

'That's right,' I said, crouching down. 'And what does mine say?'

'Rosie!' Lily said, then she burst into giggles. Oscar joined in. Honestly, what is so funny about my name? It's bad enough being called Nosy

Parker by Amanda Hawkins and her gang (I know it's my instant-messaging name, but when she says it, it's not cute, it's just cringeworthy). Now children were laughing at my real name too. I looked up at Abs for some help.

Abs shrugged her shoulders and followed Jeff and Soph down a corridor. Soph was striding along next to Jeff – obviously having a word about the person in charge of the wardrobe. I grabbed Lily and Oscar's hands and we all went to Jeff's dressing room.

It was a nice large room with lots of sofas and mirrors in it. Lily and Oscar immediately rushed up and pulled faces in the mirrors. Jeff disappeared to the loo to change and we arranged ourselves on the comfy sofas.

'OK, I'm due on set now,' Jeff said, reappearing in a purple shirt and looking at his watch. 'You can watch the show on this telly here. Make sure you don't let the children out of your sight, won't you?'

'Of course,' we all said, nodding.

'See you in an hour or so.' He kissed his children and went off.

We looked at each other.

'Let's explore!' I said.

'Explore!' Oscar said.

'Oscar, you must be a good boy,' Lily told him.

'Yes,' he said, nodding furiously.

'Come on then,' Soph said, practically out of the door already. 'I reckon the wardrobe department's this way.'

Top five reasons not to go exploring in a TV studio with small children:

1. They can run REALLY fast down corridors. I mean, I do PE every week, but you have to be some kind of Olympic athlete to keep up with a five-year-old and three-year-old.

2. They always want to go through the door with the red light above it that says 'Recording'. We got lots of stern looks from bouncer-type blokes just inside those doors.

3. You get stuck with boring people who work in the studio and who talk to the cute children for ages, when all you want to do is bump into some celebs.

4. Just when you think you've spotted someone famous, they decide they need a wee, so you have to go and find the loo.

5. One of them will go missing and you will seriously panic.

'Rosie, where's Oscar?' Abs suddenly said. We were still on Soph's mission to find the wardrobe department and I'd been distracted briefly by a framed photo on the wall of Mirage Mullins singing on a chat show. She looked great, as per usual. I'd been wondering if we'd ever see her again. It wasn't likely. An internationally famous pop star wouldn't really have time to catch up with three girls from Borehurst who once helped her out, even if she wanted to. When I came back to reality, Oscar had disappeared.

'He was just here a minute ago!' I flapped.

'He can't have gone far,' Abs reasoned, grabbing hold of Lily's hand so we wouldn't lose her too. 'We'll just have to knock on every door.'

'Jeff's going to kill us!' Soph said, her eyes wide.

'Come on then!' I said, and knocked on the nearest door.

'Yes?' said a voice from inside.

'Erm, has a three-year-old boy just run in there?' I asked.

'No,' the voice replied.

I ran to the next door, hoping we'd find him soon. We *had* to find him soon.

Ten doors later, we were getting *really* worried. Seriously, I didn't realise TV studios were so large. And so full of hiding places.

'Oscar!' shouted Lily.

'Oscar!' we all yelled.

I knocked on another door. 'Excuse me,' I called. 'Has a three-year-old boy run in there, please?'

'I'm free and a *half*,' said a voice. Oscar! I pushed the door open and ran in, to see Oscar sitting on a chair, laughing, next to Estelle. Soph and Abs and Lily ran in after me.

'Oh, Estelle!' I said, intelligently. Ooh, la, la! It was only our fave contestant from the show!!!

'Hi,' she replied, looking a bit confused at the sight of four panicked people legging it into her dressing room.

'Sorry to disturb you,' I said. 'We lost Oscar, you see. We'll go now – I'm sure you don't need strangers in your dressing room just before you go out to perform! Ha, ha! I know I wouldn't. You know. If I was going to perform. Which I'm not. Erm, anyway . . .' *Great, Rosie, just babble on. She must think you're completely mad.*

Soph grabbed Oscar and we all turned to leave.

'Hey, don't take away my youngest fan!' Estelle said, laughing. 'We were just having a nice chat, weren't we, Oscar?'

'I like cats,' he announced.

Estelle laughed again. 'Yeah, I like cats too. Come in, please, all you guys.' She gestured to the sofa in the corner. 'I could do with some more Oscar chat before going on stage. I'm, like, so nervous!'

Wow! We were going to chat to Estelle from *Stage-Struck*!

'OK. Thanks!' Abs said, leading Lily to a chair. Lily was gazing at Estelle in awe. She did look amazing – she was wearing a green, strapless chiffon dress, with sparkly bits on the hemline.

'Is that Pelligrano?' asked Sophie, looking closely at her dress.

'I dunno,' Estelle said. 'I just wear what they tell me to wear, y'know? It's lovely, isn't it? I've never had anything like this before. I'm normally in, like, jeans and trainers!'

'Yeah, know what you mean,' I said.

'So. I'm Estelle . . .' Estelle said.

'Oh, yeah, hi. I'm Rosie,' I said.

'Ringa ringa Rosie!' Lily sang, twirling round and round. Oscar giggled.

'And I'm Abigail.'

'And I'm Sophie. This is Lily, and you've already met Oscar. They're Jeff's children. We're babysitting.'

'Oscar,' said Oscar, pointing at his name badge.

'Oh, they're so cute!' Estelle exclaimed.

'It must be really exciting being on this show,' Abs said.

'Oh, yeah.' Estelle beamed. 'It's just awesome! I mean, I've never done anything like this before. It's, like, what I've always dreamed of!'

'So you've never done any singing before?' I asked.

'No, well, yeah, I mean I sing *all* the time at home and at work. They get really annoyed at work, though of course now they're lovin' it cos they're getting publicity.' Estelle smiled at us, and glanced at the children, who were playing with the cuddly toys Estelle had on her table, her chairs – well, everywhere really. Oscar was making a teddy bear dive off chairs and land 'splat' on the floor.

'Oh, yeah, they filmed you there a few weeks ago, didn't they?' Soph said.

'Yeah. I so can't wait to get out of that place. Can't stand burgers. I'm a vegetarian – can you believe it?! But it was the only job there was. It totally sucks.'

'I thought my job in a beauty salon was bad,' Soph said.

'I tell you – if I get this part in *High Kickin'* it will mean so much to me. And my mum. She's worked so hard for me all her life. I'm like, I want to repay her, you know? And you can't do that working in a burger joint!' Estelle laughed again.

As I listened to Estelle, I thought I heard a slight twang in her voice. 'Have you always lived in England?' I asked her.

'Nope. Me and Mum came to Britain from America a few years ago. I lived there till I was fifteen. In New England.' Estelle pointed to a photo in the corner of the mirror above her dressing table. Me, Abs and Soph all looked at it. It was of Estelle and a woman standing outside a white wooden house, laughing. It looked très windy there – they were almost being blown off their feet.

Just then, someone knocked on the door and a woman stuck her head round it.

'Hi, Mum!' Estelle said. 'This is my mum, Diane.'

'Hi, honey,' the woman said. She smiled at us all. 'Who are all of these people, Estelle?'

'These are Jeff Dalglish's children, and this is Rosie, Abigail and Sophie. They're babysitting. They're helping me forget my nerves!'

Diane came into the room. She looked a lot like Estelle – slim, with dark hair, but with a thick fringe. She looked très young to have a teen daughter, I couldn't help thinking.

'Thanks so much for keeping Estelle busy, you guys,' she said. She had a similar twang to Estelle. 'I got talking to some of the other mums, down in make-up, and, well, you know how it is. You get chatting, then you find you've lost all track of time and you've abandoned your baby for hours!' She grinned fondly at Estelle.

'Hello, I'm Lily,' said Lily, looking up seriously.

Diane smiled back. 'Hi there!' she said softly. 'Nice to meet you sweetie.' Lily grinned.

'You must be so proud of your daughter,' I said. 'She's fantastic! We've been voting for her every week!'

Diane smiled. 'Thanks, girls! It's so nice to meet some of Estelle's fans. It's all been so amazing – we're overwhelmed by people's response, aren't we, honey?'

Estelle nodded, grinning at us.

'And yes, I'm incredibly proud of my wonderful daughter,' Diane said.

'Are you going to sit in your usual seat tonight, Mum? I'll look out for you!' Estelle said, looking a bit embarrassed by her mum's gushing, even though it was completely justified in my view.

'Yup. I just popped by to say good luck! Knock 'em dead, kiddo!' She kissed Estelle on the cheek. 'Bye everyone! Nice to meet you!'

'Bye!' Oscar shouted, waving wildly.

'Bye!' we all chorused, as Diane left to go and sit in the audience.

'Your mum's really nice,' I said to Estelle.

'Yeah, she is,' she said, looking at Oscar and Lily. 'If you have nice parents, you're so lucky, I think. I reckon these two have nice parents. Jeff is so cool and so down-to-earth.'

'Yeah,' Soph said. 'He's so kind and friendly, you'd never know he was really famous.'

Estelle nodded. 'I'd be honoured to work with him if I won. He'd be such a good mentor. I mean, he's so grounded. I guess it's cos of his childhood.'

I nodded vigorously. 'Yeah, I read that article in *Star Secrets*, too,' I said. 'The one where he revealed all about his sad upbringing and his long-lost sister. It was amazing he was so open about it. That's why I love that magazine – it always gets the best scoops!'

'Rosie's even worked for it, haven't you, Rosie?' Soph said. 'She did work experience there for a while and the editor still asks her to write the odd article.'

'Really?' Estelle looked a bit startled. Alarmed, even.

Just then, there was a knock at the door. 'Estelle Mayor to the studio floor please. Estelle to the floor.'

Estelle leaped up. 'I'm on! Gotta go!' She

rushed out of the door, but not without casting a worried glance back at me.

Weird. What was *that* about?

Chapter Six

We went back to Jeff's dressing room to watch the rest of the show. We didn't dare go any closer to the actual studio, in case Oscar ran off again. Imagine if he ran in front of a camera! That would be très embarrassing. Anyway, it was comfy in Jeff's room, plus he'd got toys to keep the kids amused. But it was so weird thinking that we were only a few metres away from where the contestants were singing their hearts out!

'And now, Estelle Mayor, singing "I Will Never Forget You"!' said Daisy Finnegan. The audience went wild for a few seconds but as soon as the music started up, they went quiet to hear Estelle singing. Only, maybe they shouldn't have bothered.

'Is it me, or does that sound a bit wrong?' Soph asked, wincing at a high note.

'Si, si, signor. She's not normally this flat, is she?' I replied.

'Maybe she's really nervous,' Abs suggested.

But I didn't think that was all. She didn't look happy, when normally her performance would have been full of T and E (teeth and eyes in stage-school speak) and pizzazz. OK, it was a sad song, but Estelle wasn't putting her heart into it this week. And she couldn't afford to give a bad performance – she could be voted off! And her dream would be shattered!

'Thank you, Estelle,' Daisy said. 'Now, judges, opinions, please! Anna?'

'Well, I was disappointed, frankly,' Anna began, then she was drowned out by boos from the audience.

'Boooooo!' said Oscar, joyfully. 'Boooo! Booooo!'

'Ssssh,' said Lily. 'It's Daddy now.'

'I think you're capable of better, Estelle,' Jeff began. The boos were a bit shorter this time. 'I know you are, in fact. What happened? Your pitch was off, you looked distracted, it seemed like you'd only sung that song once before in your life. You can't afford to behave like this in a West End show, you know. We need dedicated, focused professionals who are going to put in one hundred per cent every night.'

Estelle looked tearful, but nodded bravely. Daisy had a sympathetic arm round her shoulders.

'And you, Michael?' Daisy said.

'I agree with the others,' Michael said. 'If you don't shape up, you can ship out!' There were loud boos and hisses at this. Estelle's eyes were now brimming with tears.

'OK!' said Daisy. 'Well, luckily it's not up to them to decide, it's up to you! So get voting. We'll be back after this break.'

'Oh, dear,' Abs said. 'Poor Estelle.'

'Boo! Boo! Boo!' Oscar was chanting, running round and round the dressing room.

'When's Daddy coming to get us?' Lily asked. 'Are we going home soon?'

We spent the next hour entertaining the children, trying to watch the rest of the show at the same time. I had to stand in front of the door so that Oscar couldn't run out of it and disappear again. He kept trying to get round me. It was very difficult to watch the TV while foiling the plans of an energetic small child, but I saw most of the show, or heard it anyway. Everyone else was as good as the week before – it was only Estelle who'd taken a surprising nosedive. Bizarre.

When it finished, we got the children into their coats and waited for Jeff to come and get us. Oscar was very sleepy now, although he insisted he wasn't, and Lily was getting a bit whiny about where Daddy was. I thought I'd just stick my head out into the corridor to see if Jeff was coming. And guess who came rushing past, sobbing? Yes, siree – Estelle!

I popped back into the room. 'Estelle's upset. Going to check she's OK. Back in a sec,' I gabbled to Soph and Abs, who looked a bit surprised. Then I zoomed off after Estelle. She looked like she needed a friend to say something encouraging. After all, we knew she could do it – she was just having an off day, that was all.

I knocked on Estelle's door and stuck my head round it. 'Hi, Estelle, just wanted to say –'

Diane moved swiftly towards the door and cut me off. 'Go away! Estelle doesn't need you hangers-on. She needs some space. Leave her alone!' And she shut the door in my face!!!

I couldn't believe it! Diane had been so nice before. I know her daughter was upset, but I mean, slamming the door in my face? That was going too far. I was still standing there, amazed, when I heard some of the conversation inside the room. It was obviously getting heated. (Yes, OK, I'm known as Nosy Parker, but I didn't deliberately eavesdrop, honestly!)

'It's just not fair!' I could hear Estelle say. 'I just

. . . muffle muffle muffle.'

Then Diane replied in a très muffly way (very annoying) and then Estelle suddenly cried, 'I don't know how much longer I can keep quiet!'

At that moment, Soph and Abs arrived with Oscar and Lily. 'Come on, Rosie,' Soph said. 'We're meeting Jeff at reception.'

The door to Estelle's dressing room suddenly flew open and Diane ushered Estelle out in front of her. It was obvious Estelle had been crying. She had her head down and her hair was covering her face. I opened my mouth to say something, but Diane shot me such a nasty look I shut it again. They rushed off down the corridor without a word.

'What the crusty old grandads was that about!' Abs exclaimed. 'She looked like she hated you!'

'I know,' I said, sadly. 'I don't know why. She slammed the door in my face just now. She was so nice before!'

Shrugging our shoulders, we went to reception and met Jeff. He took the sleepy Oscar from Soph and we all piled into the car.

'So, girls,' he said, once we were on our way back to Borehurst. 'Did you enjoy tonight's show?'

'Oh, yeah!' we all said.

'But it was weird about Estelle, wasn't it?' said Soph. 'Y'know, being so off-key like that. Normally she's so good.'

'I know,' said Jeff. 'We were probably a bit harsh on her, but it's only because we know how good she can be. That's what's so frustrating in my line of business – sometimes people let these opportunities go just because they lose their concentration.'

'I wonder why though,' I said thoughtfully. 'You know, we met her before the show and she was fine. And her mum was really nice to us. Then, just now, Estelle was upset and her mum was horrible to me.'

'Well,' Jeff said, 'her mother's probably just protective of her. It's not easy being criticised every week. And the media coverage can really take its toll on you when you're not used to it. It takes its toll even when you are!'

We all looked at each other, remembering Jeff's worry about the crazy 'Jane' who was stalking him.

'Estelle's mum's probably just worried about whether her daughter can cope,' Jeff continued. 'And, frankly, I'm not surprised. Judging by tonight's performance, the pressure's starting to get to her.'

'But it wasn't. I mean, it wasn't earlier,' I said. 'She couldn't have been more normal.' I was convinced there was more to it than nerves or media pressure. But what?

After Jeff had dropped me back home, I went to make myself a hot drink. Nan was in the kitchen, running a damp cloth over the surfaces.

'Hello, love,' she said. 'Have a nice time?'

'Yes, thanks . . .' I said, switching on the kettle.

There was a pause, then Nan said, 'Rosie? Are you sure you want to put a teabag in that mug? You've just put hot-chocolate powder in it.'

I looked in the mug. 'Oh, so I have!'

'Come on, sit down and tell me what's on your

mind. I'll do the drink,' Nan said, bustling me into a chair and sorting out a new mug, this time minus the teabag. 'Right then. Spill!'

Spill? She really does watch to many detective programmes. 'Well,' I began, 'we met Estelle before the show.'

'The lovely girl with dark hair you want to win?' Nan asked.

'Yup. Oscar ran into her dressing room so we ran after him, and she was really nice about it. We had a chat before she had to go on and sing.'

'Oooh, I saw that, just before I switched over to *Midsomer Murders,*' Nan said. 'She wasn't very good this week, was she?'

'That's the point. She was fine before the show. Then she went all weird and gave a dodgy performance. And afterwards, her mum shut the door in my face, when she'd been as nice as pie earlier.'

'When did she go weird? What were you talking about?' Nan put her hand on her chin like Jessica Fletcher from *Murder, She Wrote.*

'Well, we were talking about the show, and about how it's Estelle's dream to sing and dance, and about how nice it was to meet some fans. Oh, yeah, and Estelle went on about how great Jeff is and stuff.'

'It sounds like a very nice chat,' Nan said, giving me my mug of hot chocolate.

'Yeah, exactly. It was. But then, right at the end, just before she went on stage and did badly, she went weird. She stared at me in this odd way.'

'Interesting. So it's you she doesn't like,' Nan said.

'Gee, thanks,' I said, blowing on my hot chocolate to cool it down.

'And you said her mum shut the door in your face?'

'Yeah,' I said. 'It was like she was a different person, you know.'

'Hmm. Maybe she's one of those pushy stage-school mums and she's upset that her daughter didn't do very well,' Nan suggested, offering me a custard cream.

'Yeah, maybe.' I wasn't convinced.

'Or, maybe they just want to get close to Jeff and they thought you'd ruin their plan by telling him,' Nan said.

'What?'

'I saw that article in your magazine, before I recycled it. It's quite an interesting magazine, isn't it? I never knew you could buy outfits just like the celebrities wear. From the high street too!'

'Which article did you see, Nan?' Honestly, I love Nan but sometimes she does drive me mad.

'The one where Jeff Dalglish talks about his lost sister. I reckon lots of people will be calling him up, saying they're her. He's very rich, after all.' Nan nodded knowingly.

'Yes, he told us he has a sort of stalker who keeps on calling him, saying she's Jane,' I said, sipping my drink.

'Well, maybe this Estelle's mum is going to pretend to be Jane too,' Nan suggested.

I thought about it. 'Hmm, yeah – but it seems like a long-winded way of getting to meet him. I mean, why bother, when Estelle is so talented anyway?'

'Well, just remember,' Nan said, 'you can never tell what's going on in someone else's heart.'

'Have you been watching too many murder shows again, Nan?' I said. 'Not everyone's out to do harm to someone else, you know.'

'I'm just saying, mark my words, there might be more to that woman than you think.' Nan tapped her nose mysteriously.

Sacré bleu! Now Nan had decided Diane was an evil murderer with hidden secrets, and all she'd really done was slam the door in my face! Enough! 'I'm off to bed now, Nan. Night-night.'

'Night, love.'

But I couldn't sleep. Now Nan had put the idea in my head, I couldn't stop thinking that Diane was another wannabe Jane. And she could get much closer to Jeff than the other woman. And today she was even close to the children! Oh, no!

I sat up in bed and texted the others to log in so we could all talk:

NosyParker: Right, so earlier I heard Estelle say to her mum she couldn't keep quiet much longer. I couldn't tell you before cos Jeff was there.

FashionPolice: You woke me up to say that? If you ask me, she definitely needs to keep quiet from now on. Permanently.

CutiePie: Harsh. But fair.

NosyParker: Listen – they must have some kind of secret.

CutiePie: If it involves how to get back to sleep, I need to know it. Otherwise, at the moment, I don't care.

NosyParker: What if she's pretending to be Jane?

FashionPolice: Who? Estelle?

NosyParker: No! Diane!

CutiePie: Why would she do that?

NosyParker: To get to Oscar and Lily! To get to Jeff!

FashionPolice: No way, José. You're sleep-typing.

NosyParker: Seriously, I think they could be in danger. You heard what Jeff said about that woman who keeps calling him. He's très worried.

CutiePie: You're très barmy. There's no mystery here. Now go to sleep. Night-night.

FashionPolice: Don't let the mad frogs bite.

NosyParker: Oh, ha, ha. Seriously, girls . . .

NosyParker: Girls?

Oh, well. I turned off the computer and tried to get to sleep. But my mystery radar had totally kicked in. There was definitely something funny going on with Diane and Estelle. And I was going to find out what it was.

Chapter Seven

A few weeks later, Estelle was still on the show. She'd managed to get enough votes that weekend to scrape through, and then the following weeks she'd totally redeemed herself by being brilliant. Even I had to admit that she was the best contestant by far. She had a great voice, she was really nice, and she seemed the most down-to-earth of the lot of them.

Every week there was a little section on each contestant, showing them practising over the previous few days, along with their best bits from earlier shows and also some interviews with their mates and family. This last bit was always highly amusing because they often showed baby photos and other embarrassing stuff. Felipe, this cool rock-god wannabe with long hair and skin-tight jeans, had been totally embarrassed by his mum, who proudly showed the camera a photo of him when he was about seven. He looked like a geek, with short hair and a bowtie. Luckily for him, he had a sense of humour and laughed about it afterwards, so everyone still liked him.

There was always a section on Estelle, of course, and I watched this like a hawk, looking out for any unusual behaviour. The only thing I could say, though, was that while Estelle still seemed really sweet, chatting away happily, her mum practically never appeared on telly like all the other mums did. The cameras would zoom in on her cheering every week in the audience, but she'd never give an interview or show any baby photos.

One week, Daisy Finnegan asked Estelle how her mum was.

'Mum's fine, thanks,' said Estelle, fiddling with her hair. 'She's so excited for me.'

'She's keeping your past a secret!' Daisy joked. 'We've had no baby photos from her. I bet you were a very cute baby!'

Estelle looked a bit nervous. 'Er, yeah, well, you know, she says it's not about that, it's about how I perform now. And she's right. I need to show the judges I can do it!'

'I'm sure you will,' Daisy said. 'What are you singing this week?'

'I'll be singing "Ain't No Love like Yours", Daisy.' Estelle had perked up a bit now, and she went on to explain how she was finding it hard to get the timing right on this one.

Despite Estelle going a bit weird every time her mum was mentioned, Soph and Abs refused to believe anything was up. I was forced to discuss my worries with Nan. She agreed with me – there was definitely something going on. But then, she's always suspicious, just like Jessica Fletcher. 'It pays to be vigilant, Rosie,' Nan kept saying. 'Mark my words.'

The Tuesday before the final of *Stage-Struck* there was another article about Jeff in *Star Secrets*. Well, it wasn't so much an article about him as a news item about his latest crazy stalker. There was a picture of him and Melissa walking near their house looking harassed, with the kids. (The kids' faces were blurred out, which was a good thing. That way no one could recognise them and kidnap them. Although *Diane* knew what they looked like, I couldn't help thinking . . .)

On the facing page there was a picture of the woman who'd pretended to be Jane. I'd tried to read the article at school, but Amanda Hawkins had appeared from nowhere and started going on about me and my 'imaginary' celeb friends again, so I put *Star Secrets* away until later that afternoon. Then, when we were in Soph's bedroom after school, I showed the girls.

'I can't believe this woman thought putting some make-up on her forehead would convince Jeff she was his sister!' Abs said, amazed.

'Au contraire, mon frère. It's incredible what

you can do with make-up nowadays,' Soph said, flicking through a copy of *Vogue* to show us some fantastic new look.

'Hel-*lo*? Having flawless skin from some new foundation is a little different to faking a birthmark!' I said.

''Spose,' Soph said. She pulled out her lipgloss. It must have been some kind of automatic response to this talk of make-up. I must try that on her in a maths lesson one day.

'Look at her!' Abs said, pointing at the fake Jane's picture. She was pouting and wearing a really inappropriate outfit. (The woman, that is, not Abs.) 'She doesn't even look sorry!'

Soph peered over my shoulder. 'Yes, well, you can tell she's desperate to get in the papers. Look at that short skirt.' As per usual, Soph reckoned she could tell what this woman was like from what she was wearing. Frankly, I think you have to talk to someone to know what they're like. Although, in this case, Soph had a point. The woman was certainly milking her fifteen minutes of fame, even if she *had* been exposed as a fraud.

'I wonder how the Dalglishes are taking it,' Abs said.

'It must've been gutting to think you'd found your sister and then realise she's a fake,' I said. 'He actually met up with this one as well, it says!'

Just then, Soph's home phone rang and we listened as her mum answered it downstairs. Then she called up. 'Soph! It's for you! Jeff Dalglish wants to know if you'll babysit this weekend?'

Soph nearly swallowed her lipgloss. 'Coming!' she yelled, hurtling out of the room.

Me and Abs looked at each other. How bizarre. Just as we were talking about him. We waited impatiently for Soph to return. Five minutes later, she was back, charging through the door and panting at us.

'Saturday. Studio. Babysit,' she said, jumping up and down.

Abs and I leapt up and jumped up and down too. Saturday was the final of *Stage-Struck*!!! And we were going to be at the studio!!! Coolissimo!!

That Saturday, we all went to Jeff's house again. Melissa was on another job (lucky her, filming in Hawaii with that gorgey actor from the soap *Honeydale*!) and Oscar and Lily were overjoyed to see us. Particularly Oscar, who ran round me in circles singing, 'Ringa ringa Rosie, we all fall down,' and then collapsing in a heap and giggling.

Jeff was even more tense than before – he hardly spoke to us – so I didn't dare mention my suspicions about Diane and Estelle. I had no evidence, after all, and I didn't want to make his mood even worse. Anyway, how could I tell him there was something strange going on when I had no idea what it might be?

Me, Soph and Abs had made a pact to keep Oscar and Lily beside us at all times. The last thing we wanted to do was give Jeff – or us – any more stress! And we wanted to watch the whole programme – you know, BECAUSE IT WAS

THE FINAL!!! – so we couldn't afford to waste time running about after them.

'Since you've done such a great job taking care of these two,' Jeff said, when we were on the way to London, 'I'll arrange for you to watch this final show from the wings, just off the set. That way you can be right in the thick of it, feeling the tension with us all!'

'Great! Thanks!' we all said.

'Are you sad it's all coming to an end?' I asked him.

'Oh, no! I mean, I've enjoyed it in a way, and I think we've found some very talented performers, but I will be very glad to get back to the day job and get out of the papers.' He gave a wry smile and then fell silent again.

When we got to the studio, Jeff went straight in to make-up and left us to make our way to his dressing room. There was half an hour before the show started and we would be in the way if we stood in the wings all the time. There were tense contestants and production people rushing about in the corridors, panicking and shouting at each other, so we played tea parties with Lily and Oscar for a while. Oscar found it very funny to keep knocking everything over, but Lily wasn't amused. We had to spend a lot of time stopping her from hitting him. I was suddenly glad I didn't have a brother, sweet as Oscar was.

'Need a wee!' Oscar suddenly announced.

'I'll take him,' Soph said.

'Don't go looking for the wardrobe department, will you, Soph?' Abs said. 'Just cos we didn't find it last time.'

'What do you take me for?' Soph said, pretending to be hurt. She grabbed Oscar's hand and left the room.

Five minutes later, she was back. Alone.

'He's gone again!' she said. 'I was just trying to get him to wash his hands when he scarpered.'

'You lie!' I said, not believing she'd lost him AGAIN.

'Seriously!' she said. 'Come and help me look!'

Me and Abs leaped up and grabbed Lily's

hands. We all raced out into the corridor. I was getting déjà vu.

'I wanna drink tea!' Lily wailed as we dragged her along from door to door again.

'We can't drink tea without Oscar!' I said brightly. 'Let's find him first. It's like hide-and-seek!'

Lily brightened at that. 'Coming, Oscar! Ready or not!' she yelled.

We pelted down the corridor, knocking on doors and sticking our heads in all the rooms. They were mostly empty because the show had just started, so everyone was either in the audience, or waiting nervously for their turn to perform. Typical! The final of the most exciting live show in living memory had already begun – with only three contestants left! – and we were running around trying to find a toddler.

'I'll just check Estelle's room,' Abs said when we got to it. She knocked nervously and then, getting no reply, went in.

I stuck my ear to the door, but couldn't hear

anything. Soph was next to me, holding Lily's hand. 'Why don't you check that room?' I suggested, pointing to the one next door. Soph nodded and went to do just that.

After a minute or so of no sound from the room, and no sign of Abs, I started to worry. Where *was* Abs? What was taking her so long? Maybe Diane was in there and she'd kidnapped her!

I bravely opened the door and stuck my head round it . . .

. . . only to see Abs standing in the middle of the room, holding Oscar's hand, and looking at the coat rack.

'Abs?' I said.

She jumped and whirled round with her hand on her heart. 'Whoa, you scared me!' she said.

'What's the story, Rory? Why're you just standing there?'

'Well, I found Oscar. Voilà!' She raised his hand to show me. Like I couldn't see the naughty boy who was grinning at me. 'And then I thought, hmm, since Estelle's on stage, why not look for clues about why she went all weird that time?'

'Aha!' I said, coming into the room. 'So you *do* believe me?'

'Well, you know,' Abs said, looking shifty. 'It's not like I came here on purpose to look for clues, but since Oscar led me in here . . .'

'I'll help you,' I said promptly. 'Hang on a sec.' I stuck my head around the door to talk to Soph, who'd reappeared in the corridor. 'We've got him. In here. Just going to have a quick look round. You two wait here and let us know if anyone comes.'

Soph nodded and crouched down to talk to Lily. I went back into the dressing room and started to look at the billions of cuddly toys Estelle had everywhere. Maybe there was a clue there.

Abs was doing the same, while Oscar bashed two stuffed owls together for some reason. Boys are weird. Still, at least we knew where he was.

'Trouble is, we can't move anything, or they'll know we've been snooping. I mean, looking,' I said.

'Yeah,' Abs said. 'It's tricky.'

'Trickissimo,' I said after a few more minutes of

scanning the room. 'OK, let's go then. Come on, Oscar.' I pried the owls out of his hands and held on to him firmly.

As we walked past Estelle's mirror, I glanced again at the photo stuck to the corner. Diane and Estelle were having such a laugh in it. What a contrast to the last time I'd seen them! I peered a little closer, thinking how extremely windy it was in New England, when I noticed something. Diane's fringe had been blown out of the way. And there was a mark on her forehead!!! I leaned even closer.

'Rosie! What're you doing?' Abs hissed. 'Come on! We've got to leave!'

'No way, José!!!' I said. 'Look at this!' I pointed at the photo. 'Diane's got a heart-shaped birthmark on her forehead!'

'What?' Abs said, rushing over. 'You're right!' she gasped.

I ran to the door. 'Soph! Come in here! You've got to see this!'

Soph and Lily came into the room. 'What?' Soph asked.

Lily's eyes lit up at the sight of all the cuddly toys.

'Look!' I said. 'Diane's got the birthmark! I was right!'

'No, you weren't,' Abs said. 'You said she was *pretending* to be Jane. But she *is* Jane!'

'Oh, details, details. What matters is that she's Jeff's long-lost sister! That's her secret! I *knew* she had a secret!' I replied.

'Oooh, that means Estelle's Jeff's niece!' Soph said, still gawping at the photo.

'Ooh, yes, and that means she's Lily and Oscar's cousin!' I said, turning to look at the children, who were fighting over the same teddy bear.

'Wow! This is coolissimo!' Soph said. We all gazed at the photo excitedly. We'd solved the mystery of where Jeff's sister was!

'Come on, let's go. We've got to tell Jeff straight after the show!' I said, reaching out to grab Oscar's hand.

'I don't think so,' said a voice. Diane's voice. I

looked round. Estelle and her mum were standing just inside the door. Estelle looked pale and shocked. Diane had her arms folded across her chest and was looking really cross.

'Oh, hi, erm, we were just . . .' Abs trailed off. Even she – with a brain the size of a planet – couldn't think of a reason to justify us being in Estelle's dressing room.

'You're not going anywhere,' Diane said, slamming the door shut.

We were trapped!

Chapter Eight

I couldn't believe we'd forgotten to keep an eye out for someone coming while we looked at the photo! Now the Mayors knew we'd been snooping.

'Look, we're really sorry . . . ' I said nervously. I was gripping Oscar's hand so hard he started to cry.

'I want Daddy!' Lily suddenly wailed.

'We'll see Daddy soon,' Soph reassured her.

Diane looked at her, grimly. Oscar was really starting to sob now, even though I'd let go of his hand.

Estelle went over to her pile of toys and started waving a rabbit at Oscar. 'Look, it's Mr Rabbit!' she said. He stopped crying and sniffed instead, making a grab for Mr Rabbit. In the meantime, Lily had picked up the teddy bear she and Oscar had been fighting over and was clutching it to her chest.

'Er, could we go please?' Abs said. 'The children need their father.'

'No, I'm afraid you can't,' Diane said.

We looked at each other. What was she going to do?

'Not yet anyway,' she continued. 'Look, I'm sorry to do this to you, I really am, but I have no choice.'

I gulped and grabbed Soph's arm.

'So, you've discovered our secret,' Diane said.

'S-secret?' I said weakly.

'We heard you talking,' Estelle said.

'Yup. Look, there's no point in pretending,' Diane said. 'You know that I'm Jeff's sister, right?'

We all nodded.

'Well, I just want to explain, before you rush off to write your article for *Star Secrets* where you reveal all my family's history,' Diane said, looking at me.

I was très confused. Article for *Star Secrets*? Moi? 'Honestly, I wouldn't, I mean, I don't –'

But Diane interrupted me. 'I want to tell the story from *my* perspective,' she said.

Me, Abs and Soph all looked at each other. 'OK,' I said.

There was a pause. Estelle was biting her nails anxiously. What *was* Diane going to say?

'When Estelle and I moved to England from the States we had nothing,' Diane said. 'I'd just divorced her dad and we wanted a fresh start. Forget the past and all that. But it was tough. I had to work hard to provide for us both.'

Estelle butted in. 'Mum had *three* jobs. Including one at that burger joint dive where I work now.'

'Yeah, well, I wasn't going to sponge off anyone,' Diane said fiercely. 'Never have, never will. We've always been independent, haven't we, Stel?'

Estelle nodded.

'Didn't you have any other family in America?' I asked.

'Nope.' Diane shook her head. 'I only found out I was adopted after my parents died, and I didn't have any siblings. Or so I thought.'

'And now you've got a brother!' I said joyfully.

'Get off!' Lily yelled at Oscar, who was bashing her teddy with Mr Rabbit. *Well done, Oscar. Great advert for having a brother.* Soph separated them.

'All I knew was my birth name,' Diane said. 'I didn't know I had a brother as well. I meant to research my family when I got to the UK, but I was so busy working, you know? And, well, I'd got Estelle and she'd got me. And we were happy, weren't we?'

'Yeah,' Estelle said softly.

'And when she made it into this contest I was just so proud, I thought I'd burst.'

Estelle sniffed.

'We couldn't believe it, could we? All her dreams come true – the chance of a lifetime! But then I read the interview with Jeff in your magazine.' Diane looked at me again. 'And I realised, of course, that I'm his sister.' She swept her fringe back with one hand to show us the birthmark. It was definitely heart-shaped. 'I was thrilled! I never thought I'd find a brother. But then I realised what it could mean for us.'

'What?' I said, confused.

'Well, imagine the press having a field day. Why hadn't I looked for him before? Why had I only come forward now? What were my motives? I was bound to be seen as a gold-digger – only after his money – and Estelle would be out of the contest. So we had a choice,' Diane said. 'Tell Jeff and ruin Estelle's chances of winning this show, or keep quiet.'

'Of course,' Abs said slowly. 'You can't be judged by a member of your family or it would be favouritism.'

Diane nodded miserably.

'Wow, what a choice!' Soph said.

I was feeling guilty. As a future journalist (I

hope!), I felt bad that the press could be such a nightmare. Look what Jeff was going through! I made a mental note only to write good stuff about people.

'So you decided to keep quiet then?' I asked tentatively.

'Yes. It's Estelle's dream and she'd never be allowed to compete if everyone knew she was Jeff's niece. So we haven't told anyone. And no one must know. No one. I don't care what your magazine says. There's no scoop here.' Diane was staring at me again.

Wow! She thought I was a real journalist! How cool! I must look really professional and grown-up and . . .

'Rosie isn't writing a story –' Abs began.

'Oh, so that's why you shut the door in my face!' I gasped, suddenly clicking. Nan had been right. It *was* me they didn't like! They thought I'd write about them in *Star Secrets* if I discovered the truth! It made sense now.

Diane was talking again. 'If you're the fans you

say you are – if you care for Estelle at all – you won't tell anyone.' She looked at us aggressively, her arms still folded in front of her.

Estelle gave us a beseeching look. I noticed how pale and tired she seemed. It was amazing no one had commented on this during the previous shows. She was obviously under a lot of pressure – no wonder I'd heard her say she didn't know how much longer she could keep quiet. Poor Estelle!

I looked at Abs and Soph. From the looks on their faces, we were all thinking the same thing: what do we do now? I mean, it wasn't our secret to tell. But then it was Jeff's right to know that his sister was here – under his nose! Should we agree to keep quiet, or not?

There'd been such a long pause, Oscar and Lily looked up from their toys.

'When's Daddy coming back?' Lily asked.

Then I had a brainwave.

VOTE FOR ESTELLE NOW BY TEXTING 8067

Chapter Nine

'We *do* care for Estelle,' I said slowly, looking her and then Diane in the eye. 'That's why I'm going to say what I'm going to say.'

Abs and Soph both nudged me in the ribs. 'Ow!' I said. They were staring at me in a 'don't-get-us-into-any-more-trouble-than-we're-already-in' kind of way. The thing was, this was different. This was important. It was about more than us being in trouble. I ignored them.

'The thing is,' I said, 'we all think it's totally brilliant that Estelle's made it this far. She's worked really hard, and she completely deserves to be in the final.' Abs and Soph nodded furiously at this. 'But can't you see what a strain it's all been on her? I mean, she sings beautifully, but she's so pale, and upset . . . I just wonder what will happen if she wins? If she gets the part in *High Kickin'*, and works with Jeff, how long do you think you can keep the truth from him? Could you really look Jeff in the face – both of you – and know that you've kept him from the happiness of being reunited with his sister all these years?'

Diane and Estelle were starting to fidget nervously.

I carried on. 'Me, Abs and Soph have been lucky enough to talk to him about it a bit, and we know how upset he is about losing you all those years ago, and about all these fake women who are claiming to be you.' Diane nodded at this. 'He's being practically *stalked*. He knew the risks of telling his story to the world, but he did it to find you. And all he's got is hassle from it. If you could've seen his face . . .' I trailed off. Diane's eyes were welling up. Exactly the same as the eyes I'd seen welling up in the rear-view mirror of the people-carrier a few weeks earlier – they were just like Jeff's.

My plan was working! Diane was softening. All my years of practice persuading Mum about stuff had suddenly come in handy!

'I can understand your situation,' I went on. 'My mum brought me up by herself and she works hard. My dream is to be a journalist, and if there was a show like this for journalism, I'd audition in a heartbeat. But I know if I got the chance to choose between fame and fortune and a bigger family, I'd choose family.' Even though my family is très annoying. But I wasn't going to mention that. I *would* choose family, though, wouldn't I? Even if certain members of that family sing eighties songs while wearing horrendissimo clothes, or are obsessed with biscuits and *Inspector Morse* . . . Si, si, of course I would. I love them, despite – or because of – their weird little ways.

Abs and Soph had relaxed a bit and were now

cuddling Oscar and Lily, who were very sleepy, on their laps. Abs smiled at me encouragingly.

'Anyway, I would forget what people will say – forget the press! – and let your family be happy. You, Estelle, Jeff – even Oscar and Lily.' I pointed at the children, who looked angelic now they were practically asleep. 'Surely you don't want to deny them the chance of getting to know their auntie and cousin?'

Diane gave a sudden sob and hugged Estelle. 'I'm so sorry, honey,' she said. 'I didn't mean to put you in an awful position.'

Estelle gave a sob too. ''S'all right,' she said. 'I know you're doing it for me.'

'Listen,' Diane said. 'Rosie's talking a lotta sense. You must do what you feel is right. This contest isn't the be-all and end-all. If you feel you should come clean, you do that. Even if it means losing the contest.' She grabbed Estelle's head between her hands and kissed her forehead. 'I'll be behind you, whatever decision you make.'

Estelle sniffed, and gave her a watery grin.

Just then, there was a knock at the door. 'Estelle Mayor to the studio floor please. Estelle to the floor.'

The results from the phone-in must be back!

Estelle looked at us all briefly, took a deep breath and went out of the room.

Chapter Ten

The rest of us all looked at each other.

'What will Estelle do?' Soph wondered out loud.

'I can't believe the results are in,' Abs said. 'She must be so nervous!'

'I bet she's won!' I said, loyally. 'But we never got a chance to vote!'

'Well, I'd better get back to my seat, I guess, to find out,' Diane said. 'Thanks, Rosie.' She left the room.

'Wow!' Abs said, admiringly. 'That was such a cool speech, Rosie!'

'Yeah, totally inspirational!' Soph said.

I blushed, very pleased with myself. Maybe I did have the gift of the gab, as Nan was always telling me. Words are powerful things, as I'd discovered during my work experience at *Star Secrets*. And I'd just used them to do some good! Way to go, Rosie – maybe?

Anyway, what were we doing standing around? The results were in!

'Let's go!' I said, rushing to the door. 'Bring the kids. We've got to find out if Estelle's won!'

We zoomed to the wings of the stage. All three contestants were nervously standing in the middle of the stage with Daisy Finnegan. We weren't allowed to go close enough to peer round and see Diane in the audience, but we could see Jeff in the judging panel on the other side of the stage.

Oscar and Lily were snuggled up on Abs and Soph's hips, but the noise from the audience was starting to wake them up.

'And, five-four-three . . .' said a camera operator, making a chopping motion with his hand.

There was a storm of clapping and cheering from the audience as the show began again.

'Hello!' Daisy said to the camera in front of her. 'Welcome back to the final of *Stage-Struck*! We heard these three finalists sing earlier – Mike, Felipe and Estelle – and you've been phoning in to vote for your favourite. Let's remind ourselves of their performances.'

The TV screen near us cut to footage of Mike singing a Frank Sinatra number. I glanced at the stage. Estelle was biting her nails again, and Daisy was having her face powdered. Mike and Felipe were both looking a bit sick. It was really nerve-racking, this whole business. They were *all* good.

There was huge cheering after the brief clip of Mike, then it cut to Estelle strutting her stuff for a very funky number. We'd missed it earlier.

'She's so good,' Soph whispered. 'She deserves to win.'

'Yeah, imagine how good she'd be if she wasn't under all this pressure!' Abs whispered back, rearranging Lily on her hip.

'But how can she not tell Jeff who she is?' I said. A nearby camera operator glared at me for being loud. I lowered my voice. 'I mean, it'd just be too hard to pretend.'

Abs and Soph nodded.

They were on to the clip of Felipe's rock song now. Not long to go till the result!

'Weren't they all great?' Daisy said, after the cheers of the audience had died away. 'Judges? Any final words?'

'They've all worked really hard and given smashing performances tonight,' Jeff said.

'Yes, good luck to them all,' Michael said.

'I'd work with any of them!' Anna said.

Daisy turned back to the camera that was focused on the stage. 'Right, it's now time to find out the results of the public vote.' She paused. 'And I can now reveal that the winner, who will have a part in the new musical *High Kickin'*, is . . .' She paused again. Estelle swallowed hard. Mike put his arm round Felipe's shoulders. 'Is . . .' Another pause. *Oh, why do presenters have to draw out the torture like this?!* 'Is . . . . Estelle!!!'

The crowd went wild, and Mike and Felipe gave each other a bear hug. Daisy grabbed Estelle, who was standing still, her hands to her mouth in shock. 'Estelle!' shouted Daisy over all the noise, 'how are you feeling?'

'Astounded!' Estelle managed to say.

Me, Abs and Soph were bouncing up and down with excitement. She'd won! She'd done it! Oscar and Lily had woken up and were rubbing their eyes in confusion. Oscar put his hands over his ears.

'Well, as you know, you must now give one final performance,' Daisy said to Estelle. 'First, let's have a quick word with the others.' She turned to Mike and Felipe. 'I'm so sorry. How are you feeling, guys?' She thrust her microphone under their noses.

'Well, you know, I'm just so proud to have got this far,' Mike said.

Felipe nodded. 'Me too. Well done, Estelle!'

'Thanks, guys. Off you go,' Daisy said,

ushering them off towards where we were standing. 'OK, for one last time, singing live, Estelle Mayor, everyone!'

The audience – and the judges – went wild again. Then everyone fell silent as the first few bars of her song started up. Estelle moved towards the microphone in the middle of the stage. She opened her mouth to sing . . . but instead, she cleared her throat. 'Er, hi, everyone,' she said. 'Um, I've got a confession to make.'

The music stopped. The floor manager waved his arms frantically at the camera operators, who were looking at each other in surprise. Abs gripped my arm.

'I'm sorry, everyone. I know you were expecting me to sing, but I've got something to say.' Estelle was staring at the audience, obviously looking at her mum. 'Um, my mum is Jeff Dalglish's sister.'

There was a collective gasp. 'Keep rolling.' I heard a producer whisper.

'Basically, we didn't know this when I entered the competition. Honestly. It's always been my dream to sing and dance for a living, and I was thrilled to get so far. When we discovered that Mum is the sister Jeff's been looking for, I had to make a decision – my dream, or my family. And I've decided to choose my family. I'm prepared to give up my dream so we can all be together at last.'

Jeff stood up and was waving his arms in our direction.

A security guy pushed past me suddenly, advancing on to the stage. Estelle glanced towards him, and then to the one approaching on her right. She looked a bit panicky now.

Suddenly, Jeff left the judging panel and ran towards us. He scooped up Lily and Oscar and started towards the dressing rooms.

I grabbed his arm. 'Jeff! You've got to listen to what she's saying!'

'Yes!' Soph added. 'She's telling the truth!'

'Why should I trust you girls?' Jeff snapped. 'I understand you've let Oscar run off a couple of times. I should never have let you look after my kids!'

'We're sorry!' Abs said. 'But they're fine. Look!' She pointed at the children, who were bewildered and about to cry. 'And *she's* your family too.' She pointed at Estelle, who now had Diane next to her on stage. 'And so's she. *Honestly*!'

There was complete pandemonium now. The audience was shouting stuff at Estelle. No one knew what to do – it was a live show, after all! The cameras were still focused on Estelle. Diane had joined her on stage and they were holding on to each other like they were drowning. The security guards were trying to drag them off, but they wouldn't let go of each other. Daisy Finnegan was hovering nervously nearby, looking worried.

'Jeff!' Estelle's voice rang out over the noise. 'Look! I'm telling the truth!' She lifted her mum's fringe with one hand.

There was another gasp as everyone in the studio saw the birthmark on her forehead.

'It's another fake!' Jeff cried angrily. 'I can't believe this!' He stormed back on stage, carrying Oscar and towing Lily by the hand.

Me, Abs and Soph clutched each other. What would he do?

When he got to the Mayors, who were looking really scared, he let go of Lily and pulled out a hanky. Estelle was still lifting up Diane's fringe, and Jeff leant forward and scrubbed at the mark. Diane winced and almost fell backwards, he was so rough. Then Jeff paused. The studio fell silent. He looked at Diane.

'We're telling the truth,' Estelle said again, into the microphone. Lily looked up at Estelle and put her hand in hers.

Jeff suddenly grabbed Diane and hugged her. 'Jane!' he cried. 'It's really you!'

Oscar started to cry, squished between brother and sister. Estelle took him from Jeff and hugged him and Lily.

I started to sniff. This was getting very emotional!

'So, folks,' Daisy said nervously. 'It looks like this actually *is* Jane, Jeff's long-lost sister!'

Jeff broke free from the hug and both he and

Diane wiped their eyes. He turned to the microphone and said, in a wobbly voice, 'I'm so sorry, everyone. Yes, this is in fact my sister Jane.' Then he gave a massive grin.

The audience erupted once more. There was clapping, cheering and whistling. Me, Abs and Soph were possibly the loudest. Jeff looked so happy. He stood there with his children and his sister and Estelle, and they all kept on hugging.

'You did that!' Abs said, nudging me.

'Well, not really . . .' I said.

'Si, si, signor,' she replied. 'You gave Estelle the courage to speak up.'

She and Soph hugged me.

Then Jeff was speaking again. 'We do have some people we'd like to thank,' he said. 'Apparently it's down to them that we were reunited tonight. Sophie, Abigail and Rosie – please come here!' He beckoned us, smiling widely.

We looked at each other, grabbed each other's hands and all walked on stage to join the

Dalglishes and the Mayors. They hugged us all. Daisy Finnegan hugged us too.

'Thank you, girls,' Estelle said. 'We owe it all to you!'

And as me, Abs and Soph stood there, waving and grinning, all I could think was, Wow! We were on national TV!!! Live! On the show that, like, EVERYONE would be watching! Look, Amanda Dork-Hawkins! I have *real* celeb friends, not imaginary ones!

Ah, revenge is sweet . . .

Fact File

NAME: Mr Tim Lord
(known by Rosie, Soph and
Abs as Time Lord!)

AGE: 53

STAR SIGN: Taurus

HAIR: Grey and spiky

EYES: Hazel

LOVES: Reminding everyone of the time he was a Cyberman in Doctor

HATES: Having a classful of drama students totally lacking any kind of talent – apart from Amanda

LAST SEEN: At the annual Doctor Who convention, wearing his Cyberman helmet as he wandered around

MOST LIKELY TO SAY: 'Did I ever tell you about the time I starred in Doctor Who . . .'

WORST CRINGE EVER: Bumping into his favourite Doctor Who actor and getting so tongue-tied he actually called him 'Doctor' to his face. Oh, the shame!

**For more fact files, visit
www.mega-star.co.uk**

Megastar

Everyone has blushing blunders - here are some from your Megastar Mysteries friends!

Estelle

I was walking into my first audition for *Stage-Struck* when I got really shy about all the cameras pointing at me. Just as I was about to start singing I could feel myself going bright red and instead of singing 'I'm a star' I shouted out 'I need my ma'! It was sooo embarrassing and they showed it on TV, too!

Sophie

We headed to the swimming pool when we were on our hols and I thought I was looking pretty cool in my funky new bikini. I dived in the water and was splashing about when I suddenly realised that everyone was looking at me and laughing. That's when someone pointed out that my bikini bottoms had slipped off and were now sat on the top of my head! How cringey!

Pam

I was at the shops with my daughter when I found this lovely beige cardigan that would match my peach skirt perfectly. So, I reached out to grab Liz and show her what I'd found but, as I did, I realised it wasn't my daughter but a complete stranger! I was so embarrassed I sprinted out of the shop and never did get my nice beige cardie!

Cringes

Rosie

I went into town with Nan and we were having tea and biscuits in a café when she suddenly started nudging me in the ribs. She kept nudging harder and harder and was whispering something that sounded like 'It's Uncle Phil'. I had no idea what she was chatting about till she suddenly shouted out 'Ooh, it's that handsome young man from The Bill' – just as the music in the café stopped! Everyone looked at us and I wanted to crawl under the table with embarrassment!

Abs

My family dragged me off to some horrific assault course a few weeks ago and the final thing we had to do was this crazy rope slide over a total mud bath. I was scared silly but I grabbed hold of the rope and, before I knew it, I was swinging over the mud and completely lost my grip – landing bum-first in it! I was covered in the stuff, and had to spend the rest of the day looking like the creature from the mud lagoon!

Amanda

I was a bridesmaid at my cousin's wedding and I was so excited; I had the most gorgeous dress and my hair looked so great it would have made a celeb jealous. I looked amazing and felt great as I walked down the aisle in front of my cousin. That was until I caught my heel on my dress and fell face first, right at the feet of the vicar! I went redder than the roses I was carrying!

What's Your Stage Destiny?

- I sing all day, every day!
- I'm always making up dance moves
- I'm a total drama queen!
- Karaoke is my fave thing, ever
- I live in my leg warmers!
- I can cry at the drop of a hat
- I've been the lead in the school musical
- I can copy dance moves in my sleep
- I love being the centre of attention

Singer, dancer or awesome actress? Find out your top talent!

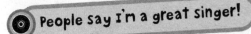 People say I'm a great singer!

 I'm always popular at school discos

I'm ALWAYS in the school play!

How did you score?

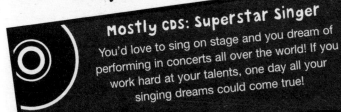

Mostly CDs: Superstar Singer
You'd love to sing on stage and you dream of performing in concerts all over the world! If you work hard at your talents, one day all your singing dreams could come true!

Mostly ballet shoes: Dancing Diva
You're brill at everything from ballet to bopping and you're awesome at teaching your mates all the coolest steps! Who knows, one day you could be dancing on stage and showing the world your moves!

Mostly cameras: Awesome Actress
Acting is your top talent and you're always faking a few tears or showing off a showbiz smile! You'd love to act on stage, and on TV, and in the movies! Work at it and your dreams could come true!

For more coolissimo quizzes, visit www.mega-star.co.uk

Astro Mates

Read on to see what your star sign reveals about your friendship style!

♈ Aries (21 March to 19 April)

You love to be in charge, so your mates are always following your lead. Why not let them take control every now and again, it could be fun!

♉ Taurus (20 April to 20 May)

You're always looking after people, so much so that sometimes you forget about what you want. Make time for you and your mates and you'll have a fab friendship!

♊ Gemini (21 May to 20 June)

You get bored far too easily so you're always planning adventures for you and your mates. Sometimes chilling out can be good fun too . . .

♋ Cancer (21 June to 22 July)

You're happiest being near your home but going to your mates' can be fun – give it a try. Organise a sleepover and see how great it can be!

♌ Leo (23 July to 22 August)

You're way confident and your mates love how everyone listens to you. Try being quiet now and again, just so your mates can get a word in edgeways!

♍ Virgo (23 August to 22 September)

You're a neat freak and need everyone else to be as tidy as you are! Give your mates a break and you could have a much better time with them!

♎ Libra (23 September to 22 October)

You're the friendliest star sign around, so no wonder you're never short of mates! Let people get close to you and you could have the best friendships, ever!

♏ Scorpio (23 October to 21 November)

You always get what you want, whether it's the lead in the play or a new best mate! It's no surprise that you have loads of loyal best buds!

♐ Sagittarius (22 November to 21 December)

You're an independent type but don't let that fool you, you still need your best mates. If you open up to them you'll have a great time!

♑ Capricorn (22 December to 19 January)

You love to do well at school, so sometimes your head is busy till break time – that's when you make up for it with gossip and giggles!

♒ Aquarius (20 January to 18 February)

You're a creative type who's always coming up with mad ideas and new things for you and your pals to do – they're definitely never bored!

♓ Pisces (19 February 19 to 20 March)

You're a shy gal, so it takes you a while to make friends but, when you do, you're a great secret-keeper and the most loyal mate a girl could ever want!

Are You a Fashion Fan?

Try our quiz to see if you're even more fashionable than Soph!

1. Where do you get all your funky fashion ideas?
a. Er, what funky fashion ideas?!
b. They just come to you naturally, it's so instinctive!
c. From magazines, pop stars, TV shows . . .

2. Your mates are always asking to borrow . . .
a. Your homework
b. Your clothes
c. Your magazines

3. What did you wear to the last school disco?
a. Um, clothes?!
b. The coolest dress that you customised yourself!
c. Jeans and a T-shirt just like you spotted in your celeb mag the week before!

4. What's the best thing about shopping?
a. It means you're not at school!
b. You get to see what's in the shops and get inspiration!
c. You can find the latest trends and get buying them!

5. Which shops are your faves?
a. Supermarkets
b. Charity shops
c. Clothes shops

6. You'd die of embarrassment if you had to wear . . .
a. Anything pink and frilly!
b. A tracksuit!
c. Anything from a charity shop!

How did you score?

Mostly As: Chilled Charlie
Fashion is sooo not a priority for you. As long as you feel comfy, you feel good! Your wardrobe is full of jeans, tracksuit bottoms and more T-shirts than you could ever wear!

Mostly Bs: Stylish Soph
Just like Soph, you're obsessed with fashion and you're all about customising and starting your own trends! You love trawling charity shops for new ideas and you always look awesome!

Mostly Cs: Fashionable Fearne
You're a big-time fashion fan and you get all the latest style ideas from your fave celebs. You've always got your head in a fashion mag and love to lead the style trends at school!

For more coolissimo quizzes, visit www.mega-star.co.uk

Soph's Style Tips

CORSAGE COOL

What you need: brooch or funky badge, ribbon

Thread the ribbon through the safety pin part of the badge or brooch so it hangs down through it (use bright colours for the best effect). Then pin it on your jumper and ta da - instant glam!

SLOGAN STYLE

What you need: fabric pens, fun slogans, plain paper

FRIENDS ARE FOREVER, BOYS ARE WHATEVER

Have a think about some fun things to write on your jumper. One of my faves is 'Friends are forever, boys are whatever!' Now practise writing it on your sheet of paper and once you're happy with it just write it on your jumper!

STENCIL STUNNER

What you need: stencil, fabric paint and brush or fabric pens

Grab a funky stencil from a stationery shop and then use your fabric paint to stencil a funky pattern on your jumper. Either stencil along the bottom of the jumper, or all over it if you like!

Jump for joy with these top tips for transforming a plain old jumper!

BADGE BABE

What you need: loads of fun badges

Collect up as many badges as you can and then use them to cover one corner of your jumper. It's best if they're all different colours. Just remember to take them all off before you put it in the wash!

TRANSFER TRENDSETTER

What you need: iron-on transfer

Get hold of a funky iron-on transfer (try department stores for these) and then get your mum to iron it on for a whole new jumper!

CHARITY CHICK

What you need: scraps of fabric from the charity shop, fabric glue, scissors

Collect lots of bits of fabric and then either cut them into letters or just into funky shapes, make a cool collage and glue it on to your jumper.

How to Be a Star!

Read Estelle's top tips for being a megastar!

1. Be determined and never give up. Even if someone says you're rubbish, get out there and prove them wrong!

2. Get on stage. Be in the school play or join a drama club, that way you can get used to being on stage and show off your talent!

3. Go to stage school. Stage school gives you the chance to learn everything, but if you can't afford it try drama lessons or after-school clubs instead.

4. Watch and learn. Watch movies, study bands and see what it takes to make it really big!

5. Be yourself. It's the one thing that marks you out from anyone else, so get out there and flaunt it!

6. Have fun. No one's going to be famous for being miserable all the time, so enjoy it and see how successful you could be!

7. Practise, practise and then practise some more! You won't be a megastar if you don't put the hard work in, it's the only way to get really good at what you do!

8. Be nice to people. If you're nice to everyone who gives you a chance then you'll get plenty of chances!

9. Work on your talents. Most famous people are talented at more than one thing. So, if you want to sing, take some dance lessons too, or if you want to act, take some singing lessons as well. The more talented you are the more likely you'll be a star!

10. Hassle people. No one ever got famous by sitting in a room by themselves; you have to get out there and be seen! So, audition, get on stage and get noticed, and one day you might be the biggest megastar there is!

BOREDOM BUSTER

Beat boredom just by using your finger and this book!

What to do: Hold your finger above the grid and close your eyes. Now empty your head, drop your finger and do whatever symbol you land on!

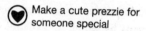 Make a cute prezzie for someone special

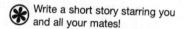 Write a short story starring you and all your mates!

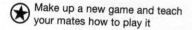 Make up a new game and teach your mates how to play it

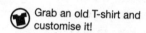 Grab an old T-shirt and customise it!

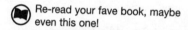 Re-read your fave book, maybe even this one!

Write your own song and perform it for your mates!

What's Your

Feeling scent-sational?
Follow the flow chart to find
your perfect smell!

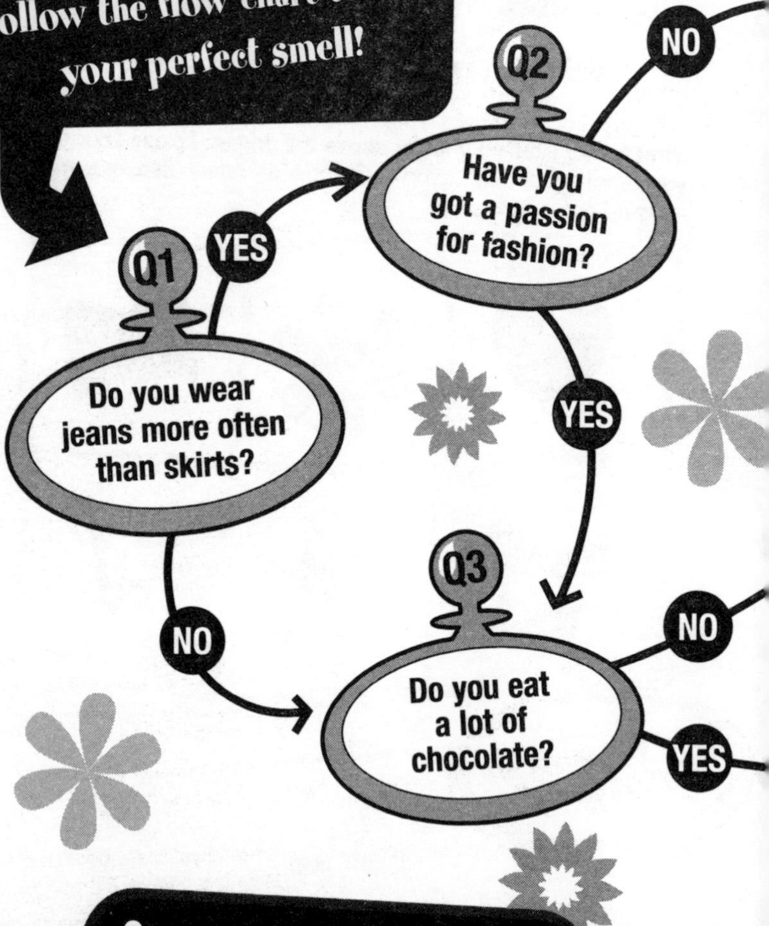

Q2 NO

Q1 YES

Have you
got a passion
for fashion?

Do you wear
jeans more often
than skirts?

YES

NO

Q3 NO

Do you eat
a lot of
chocolate?

YES

For more coolissimo quizzes,
visit www.mega-star.co.uk

Scent Style?

Q4

Do you take an apple to school every day?

YES →

Fruitie Cutie

Whether you love sweet smells like strawberry and cherry, or crisp ones like apple and lemon, you are one sunny sister who loves being outdoors. Fruity scents suit you cos you're cute as a button and tons of fun to be around!

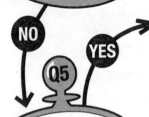

NO ↓

Q5

YES →

Are you mad about animals?

Flower Power

Girls like you love looking and smelling pretty, so the scent of a fresh bunch of flowers fits you perfectly! Friends love being around you cos you're kind and thoughtful – but you're famous for having a secret cheeky side, too

NO →

NO   **Q6**

Are you good at telling jokes?

Sweet Sweetie

Yummy scents like vanilla and chocolate are your favourite, and everyone knows it's down to your super-sweet tooth! You're always the life and soul of any party, especially sleepovers, where your spooky stories make everyone squeal!

YES →

What's Your Soul Animal?

Pick your favourite animal to reveal loads about the inner you!

If you ❤ cats ...

... you're a mysterious miss!

Fave hobby: Getting to the bottom of a new adventure

Secret talent: Reading between the lines

Most likely to say: 'Something smells fishy!'

Other soul cats: Rosie's nose for adventure combined with her love of chilling out reading gossip mags makes her a cat, just like you!

If you ❤ rabbits ...

... you're a bouncing bunny!

Fave hobby: Dancing round the living room with a hairbrush for a microphone

Secret talent: Wriggling your nose!

Most likely to say: 'I'll just have lettuce and carrots. Followed by a large slice of choccy cake, of course!'

Other soul rabbits: Rosie's mum Liz was born to be a bouncing bunny!

If you 🖤 penguins ...

... you're the queen of cool!

Fave hobby: Hanging out with mates. Penguins love being in a pack!
Secret talent: Being ultra friendly and totally cool all at the same time
Most likely to say: 'Black and white are sooo in this season!'
Other soul penguins: The original Miss Sophistication, Soph is a penguin like you!

If you 🖤 dolphins ...

... you're bright and beautiful!

Fave hobby: reading anything and everything
Secret talent: being a true friend who is always around when the going gets tough
Most likely to say: 'Who wants to hit the beach?'
Other soul dolphins: Abs is a clever clogs dolphin who always knows what's going on

If you 🖤 pandas ...

... you're sweet natured!

Fave hobby: You like to lavish care and attention on family and friends
Secret talent: Making people feel special
Most likely to say: 'Do you want a hug?'
Other soul pandas: Singer Estelle Mayor is just as caring and sharing as you!

If you 🖤 puppies ...

... you're a chatty chick!

Fave hobby: Watching telly
Secret talent: Sniffing out adventures!
Most likely to say: 'Anyone fancy a biscuit?'
Other soul pandas: You and Rosie's nan, Pam, have got more in common than you might have thought!

Pam's Problem Page

Never fear, Pam's here to sort you out!

Dear Pam,

I'm desperate to be a star and I've even auditioned to be on a TV talent contest! Now I've found out that I'm actually related to one of the judges! What should I do to keep my dreams alive?

Estelle

Pam says: Ooh, I remember when I wanted to be famous. I entered the Miss Blackpool beauty contest and I came tenth out of the ten young ladies. Fame isn't all it's cracked up to be. I think you should let your relative know you're related, dear. Otherwise it'll all come out in the papers and it might turn nasty, like something out of an Inspector Morse episode. Ooh, just the thought of it makes me want to sit down with a hot cup of tea and a packet of custard creams!

Can't wait for the next
book in the series?
Here's a sneak preview of

Hollie

Chapter One

Argh! Double maths was *so* not my idea of fun. I closed my eyes, hoping that if I wished hard enough, the numbers in my exercise book might somehow magically arrange themselves into the answer. But when I opened my eyes, the numbers were all still there, in exactly the same order, making as little sense as ever.

I sighed heavily and stared out of the window. Maths is so annoying! I mean, seriously, when did really important stars like Madonna or the queen ever need maths in real life? The queen doesn't even carry money, for heaven's sake. Mind you, Madonna's so smart, she could probably do multiple fractions while standing on her head. I bet she could explain it to me, probably by writing a totally cool pop song about it. Imagine having Madonna as your maths teacher – coolissimo! Wouldn't that be totally great? I mean, we'd probably really hit it off. Oooh, and then she'd hear me humming to myself in class one day and realise that I was actually a really amazing singer. And she'd write me a hit record and invite me to stay in her mansion. We'd become, like, totally good friends, and some magazine like *Star Secrets* would do a feature on best friends and we'd be in it. And . . .

'Earth calling Rosie. Come in, Rosie!'

With a jolt, the happy pictures of me laughing with Madonna vanished from my head, and my brain snapped into focus. Mr Adams, my maths teacher and form tutor, was frowning at me from the front of the class.

'I'm sorry, Mr Adams,' I said, sheepishly.

'No. I'm sorry, Rosie. I'm sorry if my lesson is getting in the way of your daydream,' he said. 'I'd hate to think I was boring you.'

Uh-oh. Sarcasm. 'Sorry, Mr Adams,' I said again.

I was, too. Honestly, I really like Mr Adams. As teachers go, he's pretty cool. And he's totally good-looking too – well, for someone who's ancient. After all, he must be at least in his mid-thirties. He's got really messy dark hair and these soulful, brown eyes. And he dresses OK – even Soph thinks he's got a nice line in shirts and, believe me, that's really saying something. Mr Adams is quite funny, too – when he's not making totally teachery comments. I can't help but think he'd make a pretty good boyfriend for Mum. I mean, he obviously doesn't mind a bit of eighties music, which is a must with her. I know this because I walked into our form room the other day and he was singing a song I recognised at the top of his lungs. It was by Wham! – an eighties band and one of Mum's favourite groups, like, ever. He went so red when he saw me he could have doubled as a postbox. I really think they'd be perfect together – much better than the last guy Mum went out with, Unfunny Brian. Plus, it would be just like what happens with Mia's mum in *The Princess Diaries*, which is my favourite book. Although, obviously, there would be a few differences – like, er, me not being American. Or, um, not being a princess for that matter. But hey, you get the picture.

'Rosie Parker! I won't tell you again,' said Mr Adams. 'If you don't stop staring out of the window, you can stay behind after school.'

Honestly, do teachers learn to say these things when they're at teacher-training college? Seriously, you'd think they'd come up with something more original.

Top ten things teachers always say:

1. Would you like to share that with the rest of the class?
2. I won't tell you again, it's not clever and it's

definitely not funny!

3. Would you do that at home?

4. I've got eyes in the back of my head, you know!

5. Rosie Parker! If I'd wanted your opinion, I'd have asked for it!

6. Perhaps you'd like to take the lesson instead?

7. Would you like to spend lunchtime in the headmistress's office?

8. I'd like you to have a good, hard think about what you've done!

9. If Soph/Abs told you to jump under a bus, would you do it?

10. I think you'll find the bell is for me, not for you!

'Rosie Parker! I won't tell you again!'

See what I mean?

After that, it was a quite a relief to get to English and catch up with Soph and Abs, who are both in the same class as me. I don't want to blow my own trumpet or anything, but I'm really quite good at English. Mrs Oldham says I'm one of the best in the class. Which is handy, really, cos I want to be a writer. And who ever heard of a writer who wasn't good at English? Well, unless they were Spanish or French writers or something – and I'm guessing they'd be brilliant at Spanish or French.

'Right, class,' said Mrs Oldham, brushing down her denim skirt. 'I have some exciting news.'

I rolled my eyes and looked over at Soph, who was sitting next to me. The last time Mrs Oldham told us she had exciting news it turned out a new bookcase was being added to the library. Not exactly earth-shattering! Soph feels the same way about English as I feel about maths. She was still bent over her exercise book, scribbling frantically. At first glance, it seemed like she was trying to get her head round *Macbeth*. But I could so tell she wasn't. I leant over to have a closer look at what she was writing. Ha, I was right! She was planning her outfit for the weekend. I could see she had written the headings:

Possible outfits for wearing while shopping in town:

> Day in town (sunny)
> Day in town (cloudy)
> Day in town (rainy)

That's Soph for you – totally and utterly obsessed with clothes. I nudged her and nodded towards Mrs Oldham, who was still talking. Soph sat up immediately. Believe me, you don't want to get on the wrong side of Mrs O – she's so short-tempered, she makes Scrooge look positively chirpy.

'I'm very happy to tell you all,' Mrs Oldham said, 'that Hollie Fraser will be coming to Whitney High in a week's time to do a writing workshop.'

I gaped at her. 'Hollie Fraser?' I asked. '*The* Hollie Fraser – the one who writes the *Dirty Tricks* series?'

'Yes, Rosie,' Mrs Oldham grinned. 'The very same.'

I heard Abs squeal behind me. 'But she's amazing!' she practically shouted. 'I've read all her books – all forty-nine of them!'

Hollie Fraser is H.U.G.E.! Her first book in the *Dirty Tricks* series was the biggest-selling children's book ever. Her writing's totally amazing. She's exactly the kind of writer I want to be when I'm older. I mean, she's so good that some of her books have even been made into TV series and films. And Hollie's as famous as her books. She has loads of celebrity friends and is always at celeb-filled parties. She's even been on the cover of *Star Secrets* – the only author they've ever had as a cover star. No surprise, really, since the *Dirty Tricks* series of books had been turned into mega-successful movies that made tons of money. And now she was coming to Whitney High!

'I'm sure Ms Fraser will be delighted to hear of your enthusiasm,' said Mrs Oldham.

The bell rang just then. We all gathered up our stuff and headed for the door. Me, Abs and Soph gawped at each other once we got into the corridor, totally thrilled. We had a big hug and sort of danced around till Soph realised she was still holding her pen and I now had biro all over my shirt.

'Oh, no,' gasped Soph, catching sight of her watch. 'We're late for drama rehearsal. Time Lord's going to kill us!'

The three of us hurtled along the corridor to the assembly hall where the drama rehearsals were being held. Whitney High was taking part in a regional drama competition in a few weeks and Mr Lord was treating it as seriously as if we were up for the Oscars or something. So it wasn't surprising that he was, like, really unimpressed by our lateness.

'What time do you call this, young ladies?' he snapped as we burst through the hall door. 'I hope you have a good excuse.'

'Sorry, Mr Lord,' Abs said. 'But we just found out that Hollie Fraser is coming to do a workshop with us next week! We got a bit over-excited and lost track of time!'

Mr Lord rolled his eyes heavenward. 'I will never understand why the youth of today are so obsessed with celebrity. I used to mix with the crème de la crème of fame when I was a Cyberman in the original *Doctor Who* and you never saw me getting my knickers in a twist about it.'

I heard Soph behind me try to disguise a snigger at the idea of Time Lord wearing knickers. Fortunately, he was too busy telling us off to notice. 'You know, I just don't get what's so great about Hollie Fraser anyway. She's not that good a writer. Now, my writing really could have set the world on fire. I had brilliant ideas for books, plays and even a TV series that I still believe could have been as big as *Doctor Who*, but I felt that mine was a different calling. Hard as it was to deprive the world of my talent, I felt it was more important to help shape the stars of the future, like Amanda over there.'

I stared over at Amanda Hawkins' smug, mocking face. *Yeah, right, if Amanda Hawkins is the star of the future then I'm Justin Timberlake's new girlfriend.* Behind me, Soph started making gagging noises.

'Yes, Miss McCoy?' said Time Lord. 'Do you have something to say?'

'Er, no,' Soph smiled, innocently. 'I just felt really sick for a moment.'

Time Lord narrowed his eyes at her, then shook his head. 'Right, well, may I suggest that you three make sure you are on time from now on. We have a regional drama competition to win!'

GREAT. JUST GREAT!